From Horror

with *Love*

Haunted Romance Short Stories

C. Rae D'Arc

Cover design by: C. Rae D'Arc

ISBN: 978-1-961733-08-4 (paperback)

Published by Bursting Box Publishing
www.craedarc.com
www.facebook.com/c.rae.darc
www.instagram.com/craedarc

Praise for the Haunted Romance Trilogy

Don't Date the Haunted

"Certain to have the reader laughing out loud."
– *Readers' Favorite*

"Sitting on my 'Best Books I've Ever Read' shelf."
– *Gee Liz Reads*

Don't Marry the Cursed

"Rating: 10/10 I can't wait for the next one!"
– *Leyendo.Lina (Bookstagrammer)*

"Don't Pass Up This Series."
– *Jim Doran, author of* Kingdom *series*

Don't Dance with Death

"Am I allowed to call this a perfect trilogy?"
– *Valerie Evans, author of* Wolves of Worsham *series*

"Exciting and engaging from the very beginning."
– *Libromancy Podcast*

Books by C. Rae D'Arc

Haunted Romance
Don't Date the Haunted
Don't Marry the Cursed
Don't Dance with Death

* * *

Oz's Haunting Survival Book
From Horror with Love

Dreaming Princesses
Dreaming Beauty
Fairest and the Frog
Little Red and the Lumpy Bed

To those who are willing to try new things
(especially when reading a book
that's not their "usual genre")

Map of Novel

Horror
Thriller
Mystery
Sci-Fi
Fantasy
Romance
Western
Children's

Pansy and Sean

Sitting in a Tree,

K-I-L-L-I-N-G

A Prequel Novella

Introduction

This collection of short stories is part of my Haunted Romance series. You don't need to be familiar with the trilogy to enjoy these shorts, although…

Let me explain: the setting for these stories is unique.

This collection of short stories and the Haunted Romance series is set in the world of Novel: where our fiction is their reality. *Pride and Prejudice* is a historical account of the Romance Regency, and *Dracula* is a factual history from Horror Zone.

I've said it before; I had a lot of fun writing *Don't Date the Haunted, Don't Marry the Cursed,* and *Don't Dance with Death.* I had so much fun, in fact, that I wanted to explore what happened to the characters before and after the book events. This mentality is actually why books 2&3 even happened. As a discovery writer (someone who discovers the story as they write it), I had general ideas of story events, but didn't know exactly how they occurred until I wrote out the scenes. Each of these stories was written partially to help me understand some major events that affected the main characters.

This first story is a prequel novella to *Don't Date the Haunted* (book 1 of the Haunted Romance series). As such, you don't need to read the trilogy to enjoy this.

As a prequel, this novella includes *minimal spoilers* for the other books. The only possible spoilers are in the final chapter which occurs after Chapter 4 of *Don't Date the Haunted* (book 1). The "spoilers" are vague and could be inferred from reading the book's back cover blurb.

With that said, I hope you enjoy reading these stories as much as I enjoyed writing them.

PART ONE

Chapter 1

My older brother was late, which was never a good sign in Horror.

The pit of anxiety dug deeper into my stomach, confirming that something was wrong. Being the last day of school before Christmas break, everyone had been eager to leave. I was too, but Oz always walked me home. He taught me that in Horror, it was never smart to go anywhere alone. There was strength in numbers, and one never knew when a madman or ravening beast might show up.

Actually, Hauntings usually left signs or omens before hunting specific people who hadn't faced anything in a year. After defeating a Haunting, survivors were relieved with at least six months of abatement, making Horror a relatively normal place to live ninety percent of the time.

But Oz taught me to always be alert and prepared. I even kept an emergency pack strapped to my leg with my revolver, wooden and silver stakes, matches, and other necessary items for fighting Hauntings.

I paced between the front door and the iron statue of a chainsaw—the high school mascot. Where was he?

I could almost hear him scolding me for my pacing. Revealing my anxiety was like revealing a poker hand. I couldn't let Hauntings know my fears. I couldn't show weaknesses.

I don't care, Oz said in my head, *if our drunk dad and helpless mom named you Pansy. We're Finsters, and you're my little sister. You can be strong, and you will survive.*

But condemn it all if I couldn't worry about my brother!

Oz never promised to be on time, but he was never more than ten minutes late. An hour was a sure omen. Something was wrong, and I wasn't getting anywhere by pacing.

Gritting my teeth, I considered where to go. Our places of emergency were either home or the Brimstone chapel. Home was closer. As much as Oz discouraged me from walking home alone, hitchhiking was a sure way to be mistaken for a Haunting. I had no other choice but to go alone.

I tightened the straps of my backpack, then armed myself with my revolver and wooden stake. Ready for battle, I began my lonely trek home.

I didn't walk. I ran. I ran past the guns and ammo shop, skirted around the abandoned chapel on the corner (where a wicked priest had attempted to summon demons), and crossed the street at the dojo (where Oz and I practiced defensive and offensive techniques). I didn't bother covering my size-seven footprints in the snow. I didn't bother checking around every chipped corner with my handheld mirror, which I used more to check for Hauntings than to check my short black hair, brown eyes, or small nose. I ran, risking the shortcut through the alley behind Federal Foods, Inc. and startled a black cat. Another omen.

The door to our apartment was unlocked. Condemnation. That validated my panic. Oz never left doors unlocked. I tightened my grip on my gun and stake before stepping inside.

The ring-stained coffee table was turned over and missing a leg. The booger-colored couch cushions had been torn open and gutted. What remained of the bedroom door was shredded by deep claw marks. The most disturbing sight of all was the angle that it hung.

It was ajar.

Oz never left doors slightly open. He either locked them shut (as a barrier against axes) or wedged them wide open (for an easy escape).

I kicked at the door, but my ankle twisted as the door remained in place. Ow. Was it barricaded? Heart pounding, I wiped my sweaty hands on my jeans, then re-gripped my weapons. With a deep breath, I edged my way around the bedroom door.

"Barricade" was an understatement. The dresser leaned against the door and both mattresses were stacked behind it. Their frames were tied over the windows. My older brother lay in the middle of the room.

Oz had a ring of salt around him, candles and flashlights, and an emptied pistol. Silver bullet shells littered the floor. For all the good they did him.

His body was ripped to shreds, his face half torn. I recognized him mostly by the scar above his left ear—a token from our third set of foster parents and their "pet" snake. I fell to my knees beside my brother's corpse. The thick pool of blood was still wet and bled through my jeans.

"Oz," I cried aloud, as if he would respond. "What happened to you?"

I could make a guess, but I didn't want to. I didn't want to accept the possibility. He couldn't possibly be dead. He was Oz. He was my brother. He was…all alone because I was at school.

Leaving me all alone.

No! No, Oz had always been there for me. This had to be a fake, a set up. He faked his death…and left me behind?

Nothing made sense. Oz couldn't be dead. He was my strength, my family, my teacher of survival—my *reason* to survive.

Our apartment reeked of all things awful, but I couldn't leave Oz. I distracted my senses by looking for clues to what happened. My brother had been jumpy and easily spooked since before we moved to Brimstone, making me think he'd been involved in a demonic or ghostly Haunting. I could have—*would* have helped if he'd asked. Unable to remove my eyes from the apartment destruction, I gathered that Oz's murderer was huge and used claw-like weapons. The wreckage didn't match a ghostly Haunting.

I found a little journal in Oz's dismembered desk. I flipped through it, hoping to find information about what might have killed him. Instead, the pages were filled with lists of rules to survive Horror. It was his life's work, dedicated to me.

I remained huddled by Oz's mangled body until the police showed up that evening. Maybe I called them, or maybe the neighbors did. Maybe they heard my cries. Maybe they smelled the blood from the open wounds.

The police sectioned off our apartment with caution tape. They led me away as exorcists walked in with gallons of gasoline. They checked me into a hospital, but my injuries were all emotional. The next thing I remembered was eating soup at an orphanage on Christmas Day. I'd turn eighteen next October, but the law required I had a home and education until then.

At least the police had the presence of mind to call my boss at the Brimstone Hotel to explain my absence and family emergency, because my mind was too dazed to consider responsibilities.

Most of the kids were in the orphanage's main room with the tree of lights, laughing and fighting over the donated toys.

I couldn't convince myself to join the strangers who now claimed to be my situational brothers and sisters. From the lights to the songs, everything reminded me of Oz.

A boy sat next to me. I recognized him from school, but couldn't recall which classes we shared. He had rusty blond hair, pale complexion (almost sickly), and muscles that claimed a friendly relationship with the gym.

"Hey," he said. "I heard you avoided this place for years by living with your brother."

He spoke loudly, as if grief made me hard of hearing. Still, I made no motion that I had heard him.

"Um," the boy continued awkwardly, "I just wanted to say that I respect that. You must know a lot about how to survive out there."

Survive… That word made me turn. I needed to survive. That meant I couldn't be alone.

"My name's Pansy," I said.

The boy reached his hand across and smiled. He had a nice smile. It was the kind of smile that a martyr would give while his friends escaped to safety.

"I'm Sean."

Chapter 2

Voices raised from the other room, but a quick listen confirmed the squabble as benign. Only two kids arguing about who could play with a teddy bear first, as if they had no fear of the thing coming to life to Haunt them one day. Free gifts were often cursed, but Hauntings didn't directly kill anyone younger than twelve years. Statistically, it was safe, but it was always a possibility. Oz's idea of playtime and toys was target practice with daggers.

Sean spared the squabble an extra curious glance before returning his oversized brown eyes on me. "Were your parents killed by the zombie outbreak too?"

"The—" I stopped my question as I recognized the Mass Haunting event two years ago. Supernaturals, my brain felt slow. Maybe it was from pushing back my despair, but I preferred the numbness over the emotions that threatened to implode me. "No, Oz and I moved here after the first month of cleansing."

Sean nodded in approval. "Smart. So you enjoyed the following year without Hauntings."

I shrugged. Oz and I had been nomads, avoiding our own Hauntings by moving to towns after their Mass Hauntings. Mass Hauntings struck entire towns instead of individuals or small groups, but after their eradication, the whole area was

Haunting-free for an entire year. They only happened about twice a decade in each zone, so Oz and I still had a couple of our own Hauntings. Not to mention the troubles of finding a new home, new jobs, a new school, new friends…

I couldn't help but feel guilty for keeping us in Brimstone. There had been an alien invasion Mass Haunting in Numbany. That would have moved us to Uncanny in the middle of my sophomore year. I argued to stay in Brimstone, Supernatural, for only two more years. Two more years and I'd graduate from high school. Nine months later, I wondered if Oz would still be alive if we had moved.

"Most of us—" Sean gestured about the orphanage "—are here because of the outbreak. My parents were doctors, professors from Heartford University."

"Heartford?" I asked. "Isn't that in Romance?"

"I'm a born and raised Romantic, believe it or not." He winked, and I believed it. That explained his loud and melodic voice. Did all Romantics have such nice smiles? "We came to Horror because my parents were humanitarians and wanted to study the diseases of Horror, hoping to find cures. My first Haunting was a skirmish against monkeys with mad cow. I thought it couldn't get worse, but boy, was I wrong. Zombies. They're terrifying."

I shrugged again. "Chop off their heads and burn them. They're not that different from other undead Hauntings."

Sean frowned. "It's not that simple when it's your parents. They didn't deserve to die, and they were my ticket back home. Now, I'm stuck in Horror, unable to leave with your ridiculous emigration rules."

Another shrug. I was all shrugs that day. If I could shrug away my emotions, maybe I could shrug away the pain.

"I wouldn't know," I said. "I was only four when my parents died over a bout of alcohol." As kids, Oz had called alcohol "tired juice" in Mom's hands and "angry juice" in Dad's hands. He'd been seven years old when our dad killed our mom in his drunken stupor, then killed himself out of regret. At age seven, Oz became my guardian and last family member. He couldn't really be gone too, right?

Sean's frown turned thoughtful. "I'm sorry. You're not itching to turn legal drinking age then?"

Shrug. "Sobriety is one of my brother's rules, among others." I pulled out Oz's book to look up the exact wording. Scanning through the pages, Sean's eyes went wide.

"Whoa—wait!" Sean stuck his finger to bookmark a page. "Your brother wrote down rules to survive in Horror? That's genius!"

I snapped the book back to my chest. "It's mine. Oz wrote it for me."

"Your brother's name was Oz?" he asked. "Like the 'wizard' in Children's?"

I scoffed. "Oz means 'strength.' My parents thought it was a good name for a survivor."

Sean narrowed his eyes on me. "And they named you Pansy?"

"Tell me about it." I rolled my eyes with a heavy sigh that hoped he wouldn't. "But Oz was determined to help me survive too. He taught me everything, and he wrote this book."

"That was nice of him. Could you teach me too?" His wide eyes pleaded. He wet his perfectly shaped lips, leaned closer, and whispered, "Seriously, I could use your help. Like I said, I'm a born and raised Romantic. I don't know how to be a Horror. I've been here for three years and barely survived the zombie outbreak. But I promise I won't hold you back. I—I beat a water monster last summer. I work out to hold my own, and I have some medical training from my parents."

I couldn't help but to glance for proof. Yeah, he worked out. I knew from the moment he sat next to me, but it was only natural to check whenever someone boasted about it. I easily weighed the benefits of having a medic on my side. I wished others saw me as a fundamental medical expert rather than as a sacrificial "pansy" who surprisingly survived. That would be nice…

"Okay," I said. "I'll teach you how to survive Hauntings, and you teach me what you know about being a medic."

"Awesome. Looks like we're going to be partners." He reached out his hand, and we shook on it.

The next day, I was assigned a grief counselor, and we met a few times during the winter break. The meetings were open, but apathetic. Emotions were too painful, so I went numb, scouring through my brother's book to distract myself.

My counselor encouraged me let go of my brother's burdens and carry only his legacy. I interpreted that as literally carrying his survival book. His advice was nothing new to me, but I could hear his voice between his words and handwriting. I wanted to memorize every piece of it.

Never make promises. They're only broken or kept to an early grave.

Oz taught me to be strong and to show no weaknesses. He also taught me that emotions were part of being human, and that made us strong. Except I simply didn't give a crap. Tears wouldn't bring Oz back (no matter how much I cried secretly). Neither would revenge (as if I knew what kind of Haunting killed him). He was gone. Life sucked like a vampire, and there was nothing I could do about it.

"Yes," my counselor sympathized. "I had a teacher who frequently told us 'Life sucks, then you die.' But it's mostly a matter of perspective. Our trials can help us find joy in everyday life. Suffering through Hauntings every year can help us to appreciate the peace of the rest of the year. Have you tried keeping a gratitude journal?"

For others to steal and use as blackmail against me? No thanks. I answered her with a dead stare.

"Pansy, you need to open up if you ever want to heal. If not to me, at least to yourself. Keeping a journal can help you sort out your thoughts and step back to see the bigger picture."

Again, journals were only items for blackmail, but…maybe I could write a letter to the one person who understood me. Then burn it.

After forcing myself through the first week back to school and my job as a hotel maid, I pretended to be sick to stay at the orphanage. How long could I pretend and avoid society? I slept, read Oz's book, and sat alone in the girls' bedroom, lost in thought.

Horror, why not? I'd give it a try to please my counselor.

Sitting on my bed by the window, I propped up one of my school books with my leg for a hard surface, and began to write.

Oz,

Look, I'm writing down my thoughts. Go me. Now, give me a gold star, pat me on the shoulder, and let me pass whatever unspoken test my counselor is giving me. I have enough stupid tests at school.

School was tedious before. Now, it's simply one more way to waste my time. I'm half tempted to drop out. Not like the school would worry over one more missing student.

I sat back to re-read my words, wishing Oz would respond. He'd probably tell me to stay in school and make trustworthy friends. His book said, "Don't be afraid to kill corrupted loved ones." That implied I had loved ones in the first place. Oz had been my loved one. He was gone.

You're a jerk, you know that? Leaving me alone like this. The best I can do is distract myself. All I have is your book and your voice in my head. They're my only relief from my grief.

I congratulated myself for that accidental rhyme. My literature teacher would have been pleased and gone off about the poetics of *The Divine Comedy*. Rhyming required too much thought, but a small desire to express myself grew as I continued to write.

I enjoy reading your book, the book you made for me—left for me. I can hear your voice in the words. I'll never forget the things you taught me, but I'm trying to memorize your book word for word so I'll never forget your voice.

You'd probably tell me to move on from the past, like how you never let me dwell on Mom and Dad. But...it's hard when I have no one else. What's the point of making friends? We'll all be dead one day or another.

Maybe that wasn't completely true. I considered erasing it as Sean's friendly smile crept into mind.

But I guess I met a possible friend at the orphanage. His name's Sean Chase. He's a Romantic (random, right?) and has the slimmest understanding of survival. I'm sharing your book with him, and teaching him about your rules...slowly. Horror, he asks questions about every single simple principle. He wants explanations and life experiences of proof for each point. Apparently it's not common sense to "Avoid locations with only a single bald bulb for lighting." Crazy right?

But he lets me join him during lunches and group activities. After school, we have hung out and studied together. While I teach him the basics of survival, he's teaching me anatomy from his parents' books. So much of it goes over my head, but also makes sense. I've learned why vampires always go for arms and necks, and how torturers can inflict so much pain without killing someone.

The psychology of madness also fascinates me. Far too often, good people turn to the wrong solution (and eventually turn into Hauntings) when they aren't given (or they refuse) proper help.

Condemnation, that could be me if I didn't open up to someone about my brother's death. I hated it when my counselor was right.

I burned the letter with matches from my emergency pack, then stared out the window at the falling snow, waiting for school to end.

"Is that smoke I smell?" Sean asked from the doorway after school. I looked back to confirm it was him and watched as he stepped over the threshold. A bedroom threshold didn't mean much to vampires, but Sean's crossing without invitation still gave me comfort.

To answer his question, "Yeah. I burned a letter I never intended to send."

He sat beside me on the edge of my bed and asked, "What was the letter about?"

I sighed. "My grief counselor told me to talk about my brother. I don't have anyone else to talk to, but I'd rather not talk to myself and look crazy." People already gave me funny looks when I spouted Oz's teachings that should have been common sense.

Sean gave me a weird look too, but it shadowed with a hint of curiosity and understanding. "If you want to talk, I can spare an ear to save your face—I mean, so you can save face."

I gave him a half smile then took a deep breath. I let it out slowly as I wondered what to say if I said anything at all. At least the words came easier after writing them. But how to begin? "So, Oz is—*was* everything to me." One sentence. Was every sentence going to be that hard? "I don't remember my parents. Foster parents came and went like the seasons, but Oz was with me since we were kids. He wasn't just my brother. He was my protector, my teacher, my guardian…and my best friend."

"I'm sorry," Sean whispered.

I tilted my head. "You're sorry that my brother was my best friend?"

"Uh, no," he stammered. "I'm sorry you lost all those things at once."

I sat back to take that in. "Maybe that's why it hurts so much. When I wanted to talk to a family member, I turned to Oz. When I wanted a listening friend, a mentor's advice, a guy's opinion, even a silent hug, or shoulder to cry on, Oz had been there for me."

Now, he wasn't, and I had no one.

Sean waited patiently and studied me while I figured things out. He let out a little puff and smiled. "I can't promise to be there all the time for you, but as your Haunting partner, I can try."

His genuine smile encouraged a small one of my own. "Never make promises," I quoted from my brother's book. "See? You're learning to be a Horror."

He laughed. "You are, without doubt, the strongest Pansy I've ever met."

"Have you met any other Pansys?" I asked.

"Not by name," he admitted, "but definitely by attitude. And Pansy, you act nothing like them."

I smiled at his compliment. It was the kind of encouragement Oz would give me, though he had never stared at me as intently as Sean did. Weirdo.

I gave him a friendly punch and stood. "Thanks for listening. I could talk all day about Oz and how awesome he is—was, but I think I've done enough to check the box for my counselor."

Sean's smile turned sad, as if he understood the pain I kept buried. My upbringing made it hard to trust anyone, but from that moment, I knew I could trust Sean.

Chapter 3

Over the next few weeks, our studies in Oz's book and Sean's anatomy books bled into other subjects. We studied well together, challenging one another's opinions and pushing each other to work harder. He reminded me of Oz sometimes. Sometimes this was a sweet sentiment. Other times…his friendship made me miss Oz too much.

Some days were manageable, and I'd think life could be fine after all. Then, something little would remind me of Oz, and the wound opened fresh again. One particularly difficult Thursday, Sean and I sat with our school books at the dining table. The rest of the orphans had moved to the kitchen to wash dinner dishes or went to the living room to play with the newly donated games. I had no motivation to do anything, especially to study for a physics test.

"Why should I?" I asked Sean.

"We have a test tomorrow. Don't you need to study too?"

I shrugged. "What's the point? If a murderer's chasing me, I'm not going to calculate the acceleration and forces against a bullet to determine the best shot. The kind of knowledge and skill to kill a murderer comes from experience and practice, not a book."

"True, but wouldn't you say you can shoot and aim better knowing how the various forces in the gun and air affect the bullet? And knowing those forces can help you determine the optimal bullet you want based on its size, material, and weight."

He had some points. His logic and analysis reminded me of my debates with Oz, which had two effects on me; one part was secretly happy with the friendly banter, and the other part wanted to throw back the usual rebellious teenager side that I gave Oz. So, I shrugged again.

Sean frowned and leaned back in his chair. "Well, you need to at least pass the class to graduate."

Shrug.

"Pansy, I'm serious. Don't you plan to graduate?"

"Why?"

Sean gaped. "So you can go to college or university!"

"College?" I scoffed. "Why in Horror would I go to college? It's just an extension of high school and all its problems that attract Hauntings. Also, college is expensive. I'm already struggling to save enough to move into a decent place when I turn eighteen. Why would I pay to suffer through more useless classes about science and arts that I'll never use when I need to focus on surviving today?"

Sean blinked, then turned his eyes back down to his textbook. "Sorry. I'd never thought of it that way. My parents were professors. I'd always assumed college was the next step."

I huffed. "I've never thought of it any other way. I mean, how many students were in our year before the zombie outbreak?"

"Three hundred," Sean whispered.

"Now we have two hundred, and the year of abatement is over, meaning people are facing Hauntings again. Adolescence is the most dangerous time in Horror. You want to do the math? We'll be down to one hundred and fifty by senior year, and after the statistical drop-outs, only seventy-five will graduate. College," I scoffed again. "Graduating from high school is already a lofty dream. That was all Oz wanted for me: to survive long enough to graduate high school."

Sean frowned. "Then why aren't you working harder to graduate? Don't you want to fulfill his dream?"

"Surviving long enough to graduate doesn't mean I need to graduate."

"I think it does." Sean folded his arms. "Didn't Oz graduate?"

"Yeah."

"Then you should too," he said. "He only wanted what was best for you, right? Then he wanted you to have more opportunities in life than he did. Didn't you move around a lot?"

"Yeah," I said again.

"And Oz was able to keep you both out of the orphanage?"

"After he turned eighteen and could legally apply as my guardian."

"That meant he found places to live and work. Do you really think he could have done that without his high school diploma?"

I swallowed. Probably not. He was always able to find a job, regardless of how transient we were. Oz often encouraged me to get my own diploma because it was proof of my ability to listen, learn, and complete projects.

I muttered the same argument I used to give Oz. "It's just a piece of paper."

"It's more than just a piece of paper."

I did a double-take to make sure the words had come from Sean. They were the exact words Oz used. For some reason, hearing that simple phrase made my eyes warm with moisture. Thankfully, the next words from Sean's mouth were so absurd to banish any thoughts of sentimentality.

"A high school diploma is a ticket to higher education and out of Horror."

I burst into laughter. It was the first time I'd seriously laughed since my brother's death. Supernaturals, was I allowed to be happy without Oz? Again, Sean blinked at me in surprise and confusion, like he had no idea how hilarious his statement had been.

"You think—" I gasped for breath between laughs "—that we could leave Horror? Hah! As if graduating and attending college wasn't crazy enough! You were the one to mention our ridiculous emigration rules. One impossible dream at a time, Sean!"

"But we'll turn eighteen next year, so we can get our own passports without parental permission. All we'd need is to register a completed Haunting with the Haunting Investigations Unit to confirm our abatement."

"And a crap-load of money. With my current job as a maid at the local hotel, it would take me at least a decade to save up for emigration costs. There's no point working myself to the bone for something that'll probably never happen because I'm more likely to die before then."

"Oh." An awkward look crossed Sean's face as he must have calculated my finances. "But don't you earn reward money for defeating Hauntings?"

I scoffed. "A pittance for the trouble they're worth. Sure, the more dangerous they are, the better the reward, but I agree with what Oz taught me. The reward isn't worth risking your life, and hunters always die."

"Fine," he said, frowning thoughtfully. "Then it's a long-term goal. And that makes graduating a mid-term goal. Short-term: pass the next physics test. Will you take step one and study?"

He was a ridiculous and relentless dreamer, but his smile was contagious. I rolled my eyes and smirked. "Move over."

He graced me with one of his pretty-boy smiles, and slid his chair to make room for me to study from his book.

We reviewed a whole chapter together before a shadow announced the presence of Blake Washington. He was almost a year older than Sean and I were, but in the same grade. He had the body type that looked overweight, but was actually muscular underneath the pudge. I'd seen this day coming ever since I first saw Blake. Today was the day he'd try to show us who ruled the orphanage.

He leaned to peer over our shoulders. "Looks like you're sticking around, little girly. Don't worry, no one will adopt us. We're too old, and you're too ugly."

I ignored him and flipped another page in Sean's physics textbook.

Sean however, screeched his chair back with a sharp turn. "What did you say to her?"

"I called you both ugly, but if you want to put all the insults on her, then you might as well have called her ugly yourself." He laughed.

Sean turned red, and his fists clenched.

"Calm down, Sean," I said, feigning boredom. Bullies only wanted attention, and I wasn't about to give Blake that satisfaction. Meanwhile, my mind whirled for possible reactions. A fight would create enemies, and enemies could become Hauntings. The question was whether I would fight with Sean because he defended me, or flee from the conflict entirely. What would Oz say about it? I pulled out his book to search the pages.

Sean's fist and shoulders relaxed ever so slightly. I relaxed too. Then Blake snatched Oz's book from my hands.

A small and pathetic cry escaped my lips as my insides dropped like a guillotine blade. I couldn't let Blake know how important that book was. I couldn't reveal the leverage he had over me; that I would do anything short of murder to get Oz's book back.

Sean snapped to his feet with such force that his chair tumbled to the ground.

"Give it back, Blake."

"What?" Blake jeered. "Did I take something of your girlfriend's? You know, I bet I could take a couple more things from her." I blushed with fury at his implications though remained seated, glaring fire as he continued, "Huh, Pansy? Or are you a pansy too?"

"Shut up," Sean growled, "and return her book if you know what's good for you."

Blake laughed. "If I know what's—"

Sean swung a fist into the side of Blake's face. The older boy tried to dodge, but Sean's quick knuckles still contacted Blake's nose. Blood sprayed. When Blake raised his hands to hold his bleeding face, Sean snatched my book from him, then shoved Blake to the ground.

"Like I said, if you know what's good for you, you'll leave us alone."

Blake moaned as he crawled back to his feet. "You guys are crazy! And you're dead! You're both so dead!"

Sean watched him scramble away. He swiped a couple of blood droplets off of my book before handing it back. "What does your brother's book say about idle threats?"

"Nothing in the book, but I bet he'd say they're never idle." I accepted the book back and tried not to cradle it to my chest like a little girl with her favorite blanket. "Thank you, but you shouldn't have shown him how strong you are. That'll only encourage him to bring his friends next time."

Chapter 4

"Next time" turned out to be later than I expected. Days turned into weeks, and weeks turned into months. Sean and I made a regular study routine between school, our part-time jobs, visits at the dojo, and reading through either Oz's book or his parents' textbooks.

Studying the books of our departed family members spurred some intimate conversations, so we took our studies away from the busy orphanage and to the quiet corners of the public library.

For being places filled with knowledge, libraries were highly under-utilized. Sure, we needed to avoid the books without covers (those were sure to be haunted), and the posters encouraging readers to "Get lost in a good book" were ominous, but the librarians were friendly, and the space was quiet without being eerie.

Sean and I checked out and studied books from every subject. No matter what we studied, we frequently landed on our pasts and memories. I even shared my secret insecurities about going anywhere alone—including the bathroom.

He seemed confused at first, but then I explained how bathrooms were one of our most vulnerable places. We completely undressed for perverted Hauntings that could easily hide behind curtains or cabinet doors, or be revealed by mirrors or steam. He empathized by inviting me to call him anytime I wanted an audible witness of my safety. His kindness, despite his obvious unease with the invitation, was strangely comforting.

Though our pasts had been drastically different, our futures became the same. As ridiculous as it was, I made a goal to graduate from high school and apply for Heartford University Online. Sean raved about their medical programs, saying he wanted to become a pediatrician. After reviewing all the options, I decided on a paramedic career. The fast pace of emergency aid seemed more my style.

At the dojo, I switched between the inside self-defense training and the outside range. Sean treated the outside range more like a joke as his aim went consistently wide, no matter his weapon. My specialties were daggers and revolvers, though I was hopeless with throwing axes. Sean and I wrestled together a few times before he requested a new partner.

"Why?" I asked. "Is it because I keep beating you? I can go easy on you."

Sean's pale face burned, and he mumbled, "I don't want to hit a girl."

I scoffed. "As if you could land a blow on me? Besides, we're not boxing, we're wrestling."

"Pansy," he said through clenched teeth, "I can't grapple with you."

"Why not? If you hurt me, it'll be my own fault."

"Yeah, but the positions we get into—" Sean stopped himself to turn to the dojo master, "Sensei? Please. I…she makes me stiff."

A look passed between the two men that went beyond me. "Ah." Our sensei nodded. "We will find you a male partner."

"What do you mean?" I asked, completely confused. "You don't freeze up on me—"

"Pansy," the sensei interrupted, "we usually arrange sparring partners by gender after a certain age. Perhaps we can find you a new partner who's more appropriate for your level. Gretta Hartless?" He called across the dojo to a girl who was maybe a year or two older than I was. She stopped in the middle of her spar with a girl I recognized from my classes. Her name was Carol or something like that.

While Gretta was distracted by the sensei's call, the younger girl tried to make a jab for her. Gretta blocked the attack without even looking.

"Ow!"

Gretta smirked. "Come on, Caroline. That was a cheap blow. Yes, Sensei?"

"This is Pansy Finster. She's advanced in many forms of self-defense and needs a new partner. Could you and your sister spar with her?"

"Sure thing." Gretta smiled. She wasn't the prettiest girl in the dojo with her extra wide nose and pursed open smile. But she seemed genuine, and that counted higher in my books. She shared the same large brown eyes as her sister, who skipped the wider nose gene and kept her pursed smile closed.

"You're siblings?" I asked as our sensei walked back to Sean. "I used to spar with my older brother."

Gretta's eyes lit up. "Was he any good?"

"He taught me everything I know."

"Perfect." Gretta grinned and gestured to Caroline. "Let's see how it matches with everything I've taught Caroline."

I won two out of three matches against Caroline, but only managed to hold my own for forty seconds against Gretta. We traded tips and exchanged phone numbers as friends before leaving the dojo that day. I was so worn out and happy to have new friends that I didn't prod Sean about the reason he changed partners.

The weather slowly turned warmer, and the snow began to melt. Sean and I became inseparable. We went everywhere together and called each other when we were forced apart by bedtime and showers. Others whispered about us acting romantic, but we simply practiced my brother's rules to "Never split up," and "Keep loyal friends close."

Still, a small part of me wondered if he liked me a little more than as a loyal friend. We talked so easily together, and we hardly ever argued. Was that enough to call it a Romance? He was a Romantic after all. I never had a romantic relationship and wasn't sure what to expect of it. He was handsome enough that I considered kissing him in my most private thoughts. Would it be like the Romantics said? Would he steal my breath away? Would I feel fireworks in my chest? I had a hard time imagining those sensations as pleasant and not unnerving.

I shoved those thoughts aside as we studied for end of the year tests. For the first time, I really studied. Even if my goal to be a paramedic was a distant dream, I wanted it. I found strength in that dream. In it was a hope that I'd become something more than I was, a hope that I'd help others, and that I'd survive long enough to make it a reality. Every once in a while, Sean mentioned how much money doctors and medical specialists made and reminded me of his insane goal to leave Horror. Then I'd remind him to stick to one impossible dream at a time. We needed to graduate as juniors first.

If only tests were our only obstacle that year.

Chapter 5

Blake Washington had teased Sean and me all winter and spring about being a romantic couple. He'd been easy to ignore until the stress of failing school pushed him over the edge. Who better to hate than the people who actually studied?

On the second to last day of school, I waited just outside the cafeteria for Sean to join me for lunch. He stepped over the threshold with a sour expression.

"Hey," I said, "what's that look for?"

"Nothing," he grumbled.

"Nuh-uh, don't give me that," I said. I knew him well enough that if he didn't talk about it, he'd stew in that sour mood all day. "What's going on?"

Sean released a heavy breath. "It's nothing. Blake's just an artless clay-brained, villainous fool-born, weedy boar-headed—"

"Whoa, Sean, what did he do this time?"

"He—" Sean frowned at me and ground his teeth. "He slandered you. He technically slandered me too, but he was outright crude and tried to spread lies about you. So I called him out. Then the rest of his buddies showed up. It was five against one. The only reason they didn't beat me then and there was because a teacher passed by. Blake still accepted my challenge to fight. Tomorrow, sunset, at the wild-life preserve behind the dojo. He said that if I didn't come, he'd haunt me until he chased me out of town." Sean grimaced, then met my eyes. "So, what do you think? Will you be my second?"

"Your what?" I asked.

"My second. If I die, you'll avenge me."

I scoffed. "I've never heard that before, but I'll do you one better. I can teach you all the dirty tricks of street fighting to keep you from dying in the first place. Prep your emergency pack so you can match any weapon he brings."

"I think I could take him one-on-one, hand-to-hand. But if he brings his friends or a weapon, he'll kill me."

"No, he won't," I said firmly. I wouldn't let him. I wouldn't wait for Sean to die before avenging him. I'd stop anyone who even came close. That led me to another dangerous realization. I didn't simply like Sean as a friend. I cared about him. Almost like I had cared about Oz. He didn't have my undying loyalty, but he was a good person who deserved to survive. A deep secretive and stupid part of my brain found him likable in every sense of the word, but I scolded myself for dreaming uselessly. Besides, Sean was my study partner and…my best friend.

As I mulled that over, a different part of my brain came into focus.

Something was off. The sidewalks were too empty. The world seemed quiet outside of Sean and me. Then what was that sound of scuffling footsteps?

"So, wha—"

I shushed Sean with a finger to his lips. The footsteps were too slow and quiet to be casual.

"Hide," I hissed, then grabbed Sean's hand and pulled him to the side, around the corner, and inside the nearest door. I shoved us into…the school's landscaping closet. Oops.

Whatever. If Hauntings could hide in closets, so could people. Still holding Sean's hand, I stepped over the lawn mowers to crouch behind them. A saw and shears hung on the wall beside us, close enough to grab if the sneaking being found us.

Sean shuffled down beside me, obviously uncomfortable. "Is this your way of thanking me for standing up for you? Seven minutes in heaven?"

"What?"

"No? Oh." He cleared his throat. "Um, why are we in here?"

"Shush. They might hear." Even if they weren't stalking us specifically, I wasn't sure if they were human. In that case, they were hunting, and it wouldn't matter who got in their way.

My blood froze as a shadow passed along the bottom of the closet. I held my breath and waited.

"Pans—"

"Shh," I cut him off again, barely daring to breathe. I wasn't sure who or what had passed us, so I didn't know how long to wait. We couldn't wait forever. Sean was too restless. I retrieved my revolver from my emergency pack and loaded it with a full clip of hollowpoint bullets. Together, Sean and I moved away from the mowers and up to the door. I held my hand up in the dim light to count: one…two…

Three!

I leveled my gun and kicked open the door. No one was there. I stepped out and searched the area. Nothing.

Maybe they hunted someone else. I sighed and turned sheepishly back to Sean. "Sorry. I thought someone could be following us. Anyway, what did you want to tell me?"

"Uhhh…I forgot." Sean stretched, rippling his attractive arm and chest muscles, and gave me a half smile. "You know, a lot of Romantics *want* people to follow them."

"Why?" I balked.

He shrugged. "Don't you hope there's someone out there, waiting for you?"

"Supernaturals, why would I want something creepy like that?"

"It's not creepy to be loved by someone."

To be loved by someone… What would that be like? Was it different from the brotherly love I felt from Oz? Could I feel that way for someone? Sean? We were practically siblings with how much time we spent together.

Either way, I showed Sean my concern for him by teaching him a few quick moves when grappling without rules. He would not die over something as simple as an underhanded trick. Not if I had anything to say about it.

The last day of classes was a wash. Sean and I ended up wandering to whoever's class held the biggest celebration. We watched a mad science movie in physics, filled out number puzzles in pre-calculus, read from our favorite scary histories for English, and hung out at the water station during our PE dance party (despite Sean's urges to join the dancing).

He also wanted to talk about what to expect in the fight against Blake, but I didn't want to discuss strategies during school in case one of Blake's minions overheard.

We went early to the dojo to stretch and practice at the range. At sunset, we were ready.

Blake and his four friends didn't show up until fifteen minutes later. Two of them were drunk.

The gang leader cracked his knuckles. "Ah look, the little scaredy cat brought his girlfriend for back up."

"I'm here, aren't I?" Sean spat. "Are you going to fight me like a man, hand-to-hand, one-on-one?"

"Yeah," Blake jeered. "Let's fight like men. Hauntings and beasts can fight barehanded, but only men use guns." He pulled a pistol from the back of his pants.

Oh, crap. Sean was a terrible shot, and of all the weapons in Sean's emergency pack, he was the least skilled with his revolver.

I stepped in. "Sean said that it was my name you slandered. If so, then I should be the one to fight you."

"What are you doing here, little pansy?" Blake sneered. "Aren't you supposed to be cleaning the kitchen?"

Sean was in Blake's face before I could stop him. Red faced, Sean growled back, "If she goes to the kitchen, it'll be to mop your face with the floor before sweeping you under the rug."

Blake's gun hand swept up between them, smacking Sean's nose and scratching his cheek. Sean stumbled back with his hand to his face. A line of blood now smeared across his face and palm.

"Sean," I said, "don't become a bully by standing up to one. He's not worth your anger."

Blake smirked at Sean. "You should listen to your master, little mutt. Better back away before this bullet ends up bloodying your pretty face."

One swift motion leveled my revolver to the bridge of Blake's nose. "Blake, surprise me for once, and don't be stupid. No one needs to die today."

His beady eyes took note of my gun, aim, handling technique, and posture. He snorted. "What's the fun in that, little pansy? I wanna see how ugly you cry when your boyfriend dies."

Sean growled, but I grabbed his wrist to hold him. I snapped back, "I will kill you if I have to. If you're stupid enough to aim your daddy's guns at us, then I say let's take a walk in the park. We'll let all of you play so long as you give us a ten-minute head start."

Blake grinned. "Five minutes."

"There are five of you and only two of us. You have a 175% advantage, so multiply that to the Haunting Investigation Unit's standard five-minute advantage for Horrors, and you need to give us a minimum of seventeen minutes."

Blank stares and confused blinks responded.

"Meh." Blake shrugged. "You're dead anyway. Ten minutes. Starting now." He raised his gun and fired a single bullet.

Chapter 6

Blake's shot echoed into the sky. I ran and pulled Sean behind while telling him, "Keep watch that they don't shoot us in the back or follow."

"Sure," Sean said, his voice wavering. "What was that about the 175% advantage and standard five minutes?"

"Total gibberish." I weaved us around the trees of the park behind the dojo. It was less of a park and more like an acre of wildlands. The occasional cigarette butt and fast food litter testified of a homeless person in residence. "I figured if I threw math and technical terms at them, they'd take my word for it. You can't argue with nonsense."

Sean chuckled. "You're a genius. Also, did you notice Blake already used one of his bullets?"

"You can keep count, but who's to say they don't have spare magazines? Do you have extra bullets in your pack?"

"I have six hallowpoints, three silver, and three gold."

"Me too," I said. "That gives us twenty-four bullets and our other weapons to cripple five guys. The arms are hardest to aim for, but if we take out their arms, they can't shoot at us."

"I know," Sean huffed.

The sinking sun left us in twilight, but I didn't pull out my flashlight yet. The beacon of light would only give away our position to Blake and his minions.

Sean's eyes went up to the canopy. "These trees aren't very good for climbing or hiding. We'd be sitting ducks up there."

I agreed. "We can set a trap and hide behind ferns."

"What kind of trap? We don't have shovels to dig a hole or rope to create a trip wire."

"If we can find something shiny to lure them to a certain spot, we can cripple them while they're distracted."

"Sounds good," Sean said. "I think there was an empty soda can back this way. We can shine one of our flashlights on it."

"Great idea," I said, and followed him a few steps to the side to widen the search.

Sean wrapped his hand around his flashlight's nozzle before clicking it on. His light shone in a narrow beam, and the inside of his hand glowed red like he bled light.

We were well into the park now. We took a left turn somewhere to end up closer to the East side, which was bordered by another street and fenced houses beyond. If worse came to worst, we could escape and seek refuge at one of the neighboring houses.

A woman's scream pierced the air, announcing the night like a twisted rooster call. The screams were too close for comfort, though ten miles away would be too close for comfort. I prayed to the Supernaturals that the Haunting chasing the screamer would leave us alone. Blake and his minions were enough to handle already.

"Holy Horror!" Sean swore in a strained whisper.

"What?"

"Pansy, come here."

Five steps took me to his side. Another three steps would put me standing on a body.

The twilight and Sean's flashlight revealed a man lying prostrate on the ground. For a moment, I was back in my old apartment, staring at Oz's corpse. The man in the park had the same bloody mutilation. His clothes were torn to ribbons and were dyed with dried blood. Entire chunks of the shoulders, legs, and buttocks were missing. Thank the Supernaturals, he lay on his stomach with his face turned away.

"Condemnation," I swore. Either the man had been killed by the same Haunting that killed Oz, or Oz's Haunting had friends. What could have done this?

Sean murmured, "He must have been one of the homeless people who lived here. I wonder what killed him?"

A monster. Whatever did that wasn't human.

Sean blinked and swallowed hard, forcing down his vomit and emotions. "I'm regretting that extra serving of roast beef stew I had for dinner. If I puke, will you make me eat it like a dog to cover our tracks?"

"Ew, no," I said, tearing my eyes from the sight and memories of death. Was the Haunting still around? I didn't see anything suspicious. We already had five boys hunting us, and we were wasting time. "How long have we stood here, gawking?"

"Barnacles, you're right, we need to find a trap for Blake, then hide ourselves."

I gestured at the dead man. "If we gawked for a whole minute, how long do you think Blake and his friends will gawk? We can hide ourselves nearby and wait for them to discover the body."

Sean cleared his throat. "We'll need to make him more noticeable for Blake and his friends to come inspect him."

I nodded and pulled out my flashlight, then crouched over the dead man. I flicked my light on to quickly survey and make sure he wasn't a zombie. Satisfied enough, I set it under one of his hands and angled the light at a nearby tree.

"Spooky," Sean said.

I stepped back to analyze the scene. Sean was right. How could a man who was so dead have a flashlight that was so alive? The light on the tree was obvious enough to gain attention, though the shadows it cast were gnarled and twisted.

"There," I said. "The trap will work better if we flank them."

"How about those two ferns?" he asked and gestured to two large plants twenty feet apart.

"Okay," I said. "Let's get into position and wait for them to reach the dead man. Then we take them out."

"Not on a double date."

"What?"

"Nevermind." Sean shook his head with a little chuckle.

Confused, I clarified with, "We don't need to kill them. Simply over-power them enough so they never think about testing us again."

Sean nodded, but didn't immediately turn away to implement our plan. He opened his mouth and closed it, fidgeted with his flashlight, and shuffled noisily.

Did he doubt our plan? Did he want to make a promise he couldn't keep or say parting words to seal our doom?

I nudged his shoulder and urged, "Whatever you want to say, you can say it after we're safe. Let's go."

We shuffled as quietly as possible into the undergrowth. Fog crept between the trees as the night took hold of the sky. Both features would aid our ambush, though Blake and his friends could also use the low vision to their advantage. I cringed every time the leaves rustled around me and paused whenever I heard movement farther away. Sometimes it was Sean. Sometimes it was an owl. Another time —

I froze.

Voices.

I measured my breathing, but my heart pounded furiously. Could they hear it?

I couldn't see them through the thickening fog and darkening night, but I heard them come from behind, boisterous and loud. Blake's friends. Two of them. The drunk two. Easy pickings. I worried a little less about my hiding position. A little.

"Hey look!" one of them said. "You see that light?"

"What light?" the other drawled. Definitely drunk.

"There. No, over there, you loser. Oh, dude! There's someone over there."

"Gross. They look dead."

"That ain't the girl. You think it's her stuck-up boyfriend?"

"I already called dibs on the girl."

"You gotta find her first. Finders keepers."

"What's with the light? That's a weird lookin' tree."

"Your face is weird looking."

"Your mom is weird l—" He cut off with the sound of a fist against a stomach.

"Don'cha talk about my mom. She died proud."

"But she's still dead."

Another punch.

I aimed my revolver at the less-drunk one's legs. We probably didn't need the dead-man's distraction. They were drunk, slow, and already distracted by themselves. I took off the safety when a shadow in the trees above caught my attention. The large shadow moved among the still trees and fog.

The dark and silent mass dropped fifteen feet to the ground. It landed—no, *smashed* onto the more-drunk boy.

Chapter 7

The boy collapsed under the Haunting's weight. The amount of blood and sickening cracks of bone announced his instant death.

His friend screamed in outright terror as the massive creature roared with its elongated face. Somewhere in the distance, Blake and his other minions shouted in confusion.

"Holy Horror!" Sean cursed and scrambled from his position twenty feet away.

No, Sean! He gave away his position!

I almost couldn't blame him for his rookie mistake. Even with my lifetime of practice, the deadly monster before us panicked my heart with utter terror.

I scrambled with my revolver to point it at the nine-foot beast. It swung its muscular arm at the other minion to capture his neck in a deadly grasp. Bones snapped. As if the boy wasn't already dead, the creature threw the boy's body to the ground, ensuring every ligament was broken.

Condemnation, what creature was that strong and merciless?

It lifted its long nose to the sky and sniffed. With its nose still in the air, it broke the night with a bone-shivering howl. Another howl joined in the distance. Then another. Soon, a chorus of death sang through the night. If we survived, I knew those sounds would haunt me for eternity. Then the creature's eyes met mine. They gleamed orange.

Crap-crap-crap!

I fired off a single shot, knowing I'd miss. A shot came from Sean's direction, too. The werewolf hesitated just enough to indicate a fear of our bullets. I scrambled to my feet and reached for Sean. He was already on his feet, firing another shot.

The werewolf's massive arm twitched back from the impact. Then it grinned. The bullet hadn't been silver. The monster was unaffected.

"Run-run-run!"

Maybe if we reached the dojo, we could lock it out and buy enough time to load our guns with our silver bullets.

It was a terrible plan, doomed from the start. There was no way we could outrun a werewolf. The woods didn't serve in our favor. Sean and I stumbled over the foliage and protruding roots. When did this park become so hazardous? I could have sworn the ground was more even when Sean and I ran from Blake's gang. Now, Sean and I held hands to balance one another between slipped footing and twisted ankles.

The werewolf crashed through the woods behind us like a bulldozer. It shrugged off the shrubs and charged. Each huff and puff grew louder and closer. Its elevated breathing wasn't even winded. If anything, it sounded excited.

True terror gripped me. I was going to die. I imagined the newspaper article, "Students slaughtered when third party interrupts playground fight." Or maybe the title would be something ironically catchy, like, "Don't bring claws to a gun-fight." Either way, the column would likely read, "Bodies were found by a jogger weeks later. Waiting for dental records to confirm identities."

We were dead. We were nothing more than a couple of names waiting to be engraved in stones.

At the moment, running through the woods like a lost madman, I was grateful to have Sean with me. I wouldn't die alone. As much as I worried about endangering Sean's life with my own, at least our deaths would be quick.

"I see them!"

Blake?

Blake and his other two cronies raised their guns at us.

I yanked on Sean's hand to drop us both to the ground. One shot followed another as the werewolf leaped in the air. I rolled toward Sean as the Haunting soared over us.

Only then did Blake and his friends notice the werewolf. Blake cursed, "What the—"

A gunshot swallowed his words.

I kept my eyes up to survey the situation. Sean and I were hidden well enough in the leafage from Blake and his friends, but they weren't my main concern anymore. The werewolf crouched between us. It slashed at one of Blake's friends. A scream, a shout, and a catatonic whimper pierced the air as all three boys fell back. The werewolf sniffed the air, then turned back toward Sean and me.

Crap, we weren't in a position to run again. My legs hurt from the fall and were caught from the roll. I didn't need to look to know that Sean was cut during our tumble. He was bleeding, and blood always drew attention.

The werewolf's eyes zeroed on us.

I had maybe three seconds to spare.

One.

I ejected my revolver's clip with one hand while the other slipped into my Emergency Pack.

The werewolf crouched and began another charge.

Two.

Which bullets were silver? I needed to glance at the bullets in my hand to pick out the silver castings. But I couldn't take my eyes off the charging Haunting. My hands fumbled with the bullets. My revolver remained empty.

The werewolf leaped for Sean and me, bearing its claws and fangs.

Three.

Gunfire from ahead.

The werewolf jolted, surprise widening its eyes for half a millisecond. It buckled slightly on its left. Before I could hope that it was dead, the Haunting ran off, limping into the woods.

Supernaturals. We survived?

"Um, Pansy?" a small voice asked from below me.

I looked down, only then realizing my position on top of Sean: legs tangled, our stomachs breathed against each other, my elbow jammed into his chest.

"Oh, sorry," I said, pushing myself up.

"For what?" he asked, a goofy grin sliding up his cheeks. I stared in horror at the blood on his face. The scratch Blake had given him earlier continued to ooze. The werewolf had smelled his blood.

Unaware of his impending doom, Sean sat up, still smiling. "You saved my life."

"No, I didn't. He did." I gestured at Blake's friend, who lowered his double-barrel rifle and stood on shaking legs. The other one cradled his bleeding arm like a baby. Blake, however, waved his pistol in the air and shouted threats and obscenities.

"That's what happens when you mess with Blake Washington! You haven't seen the last of me, you mother-sucking furball! You hear me? You stay away if you know what's good for you!"

"Blake," I hissed. "Shut up. Don't bait it into coming back when it already killed your other two friends."

His challenging sneer dampened. "It—Jiro? Where's Jiro and Kyo?"

"They're dead," I said, and pointed toward the place of death. "The werewolf jumped on them back that way."

"That was a werewolf?" Sean shouted, getting to his feet. "It was huge!"

One of Blake's friends whispered, "Some can grow as large as bears."

Sean continued to gape. "My dad went on hunting trips with other professors, but even the bears in Romance aren't that big."

"Also, that wasn't a mindless werewolf," I said. "It wasn't lost in the lust for meat and blood. It killed for fun."

"What do you mean?" Sean gulped.

"Your two friends," I said to Blake, gesturing back toward the two fresh bodies beside the decayed one. "The werewolf didn't need to kill both of them. Then it left its prey to chase us. Then again, when it attacked your friend—"

The boy cradling his arm collapsed.

"Chike!" Blake jumped at his fallen friend. "Dude, it's just a scratch. It ain't like he bit you. Get up."

Sean and I ran over. It was difficult to analyze the wound in the night and the mess of blood. Sean cracked open the water bottle from his pack and drained it over Chike's arm.

"It's deep," he said. "He needs a hospital."

Chapter 8

The hospital nurses spared Sean and me a few minutes to make sure we were all in order. As soon as they were sure that Sean's scratch wasn't poisoned or infected, they excused him with a bandage. It had cartoon puppies on it.

In Chike's room, Blake spoke enough for both him and his quiet and only un-hurt friend. He unleashed every expletive from Horror and Thriller about the werewolf. He created such a ruckus that the nurses kicked us all out "for the health of the patients who need their rest."

We were directed to the ER waiting lounge, walking through plain white hallways with the occasional flickering light, surrounded by patients groaning or crying behind doors. There were no windows to reveal the time until we reached the waiting room with its stain-removed furniture and bile-colored carpet.

"How's Chike?" Sean asked.

Blake sneered. "What do you care?"

"In case you haven't noticed," I said, "we have something in common now: an enemy."

Blake's only undamaged friend perked up. "You'll help us avenge Jiro and Kyo?"

I nodded. "The werewolf has smelled Chike's and Sean's blood. We're marked for the hunt. It'll come for us."

"Then we'll be waiting," Blake's friend said.

Blake, however, scoffed. "Come on, Ren, we don't need these losers. We can take it, just the two of us. They'll only get in our way or do something annoying, like stop us from taking revenge or take the reward money. I bet that thing is worth a ton!"

Ren didn't respond verbally, but his subtle shifting spoke volumes. He didn't have Blake's confidence. He wanted Sean and me to help.

"Blake," I said, "you need more people to take down that Haunting. I don't condone revenge, but I won't keep you from it." Especially if it had been the creature that killed the homeless man…that killed Oz. Either way, "Hauntings need to be completely destroyed or they'll just keep coming back."

"On that note," Sean said, "what are the chances it'll come for us again tonight?"

"High," I said. "Werewolves only attack on full moons, so it probably wants to clean up its unfinished business before it goes dormant for a few weeks."

"Depends on the werewolf," Blake said. "Tell 'em, Ren."

Ren shuffled again. "Some werewolves also transform on the nights of the fullest waxing and waning gibbous."

"The what?" Sean asked.

"The nights directly before and after the full moon are full enough to transform some shifter-Hauntings," Ren explained.

Sean groaned. "This just keeps getting better. As if that thing wasn't already powerful enough."

"Either way," I said, glancing at a clock, "it's only a quarter past midnight. The moon will be out for at least another six hours."

We had a long night ahead of us.

After an hour, a nurse informed us of Chike's stable status. He would be fine as long as he didn't strain himself. That didn't seem likely during a Haunting, so they suggested he stay for the rest of the night. Sean nodded and stifled a yawn, waving for me to walk with him. The nurse led us through the hospital to a separate wing for regular patients. The sounds behind the patient's doors shifted from groans to moans and cries to whimpers. Sean scuffed his feet against the tile floor.

I nudged his arm. "Can you walk quieter? We have a werewolf Haun—"

He stopped near the end of the hallway, standing with his shoulders hunched and staring at the tile. Blake and the others continued through the swinging door to the lobby. I hated splitting from the group, but Sean's posture gathered courage with our privacy. His eyes raised from his feet to mine.

"Something that Blake said is still eating at me."

"Eating…at you?" I knew it was an expression, but taken literally, it sounded painful.

Rather than explain, he asked, "Would you cry if I died?"

"What?" I balked.

"I've never seen you cry," Sean said, "and we've had some pretty serious heart-to-hearts. I mean, you're my best friend, and I like you, but I don't think you'd cry over my dead body. Did you even cry when Oz died?"

"Uhhh…" I had no idea what to say to that. Like a math word problem, I needed to pick it apart and sort it out piece by piece. I didn't know what "heart-to-hearts" were, but apparently we had enough of them that he "liked me." What did that mean? That he liked me like a friend or that he wanted me as a girlfriend? He'd added that I was his best friend, like it was different from simply liking me, so…

My brain fuzzed with the possibilities and meanings. Maybe I was overthinking it, but considering my approaches to Hauntings, it made sense to approach a possible Romance with equal speculation.

Unsure what to say, I skipped to his misunderstanding.

"I cried a lot for Oz," I said, "especially in the beginning."

"Really?" Sean asked. "But I never saw you crying. Did you hide it from me because I made you feel uncomfortable?"

I shook my head. "No. You made me feel better." I never cried around him because I didn't feel as sad and lonely with him around.

Sean's concerned expression slowly grew into one of his beautiful smiles. "I'll take that. I'm still curious to see you cry, but I want happy tears."

"Happy tears?" I asked. "Why in Horror would I cry 'happy tears?'"

"I don't know, but now I'm determined to make it happen."

He grinned. I responded with a friendly punch at his shoulder.

"And, um," he began, "is it possible you also like me?"

Crap, I didn't know what he meant by that. Did his shyness suggest a desire to be Romantic? Romances seemed like they caused more problems than they solved, but the idea of Sean as my boyfriend made my insides stir. What a weird sensation. It didn't feel like my usual instinctual warnings. If it wasn't a warning, what were my instincts trying to tell me?

My feelings didn't make sense, so I reverted to my usual logic. Sean was a boy, and he was my friend. He was even my best friend. Did that make him my boyfriend by default? I'd admit that I was attracted to his friendliness, strength, and… there was something about his smile that made me happy beyond reason. My most secret of confessions would admit that I was curious as a black cat to know what Sean's kiss felt like.

He continued to stare at me, waiting for a response. I swallowed and said, "It's possible."

He smiled, a broad and glorious version of perfection.

"Then," he hesitated, "is it okay if I do this?"

"This" was defined when he took my hand in his own. I needed to stretch my fingers wide around his. We both flustered for a good minute as our hands stretched and wiggled until our palms nestled together. His hand practically swallowed mine, and his skin was incredibly warm and a little sweaty. But it was also a reassurance of his presence that if one of us fell down, then the other would help them back up. A spark of hope grew in the squished space between our hands.

PART TWO

Chapter 9

In the front lobby, there were two sets of glass doors on opposite ends; one leading to the parking lot, and the other leading to the center of the hospital that featured a little zen garden and cultivated puddle. Every patient's room had a window to the garden for a view of their boxed up piece of heaven.

Blake continued to fume, but words without action were useless.

"Blake, shut up," I said. "If you want revenge so badly, then help us strategize."

"I checked my calendar," Ren said. "Tonight isn't the full moon. Not even close. Meaning the werewolf transforms at will, any time of the month."

I groaned. "Meaning, if it leaves us alone tonight, we don't get another month to prepare."

"Goody," Sean said with scared sarcasm.

Blake sneered. "Let it come! I'll bust its brains out! I'll chain it to the floor and break its—"

"So, Sean," I said in loud interruption, "it seems our year-round preparation will pay off. We're better prepared to fight this thing tonight than if we'd been lazy bums and thought we'd have a month to prepare."

Sean's return smile shook with unease. "But what is this thing we're fighting? A werewolf? It's bigger than any stories."

"Yeah, what are you fighting?" a female voice broke into our conversation.

We all turned. Gretta and Caroline stood outside our little circle. When had they come in? What were they doing there?

Blake growled, "None of your business. Piss off."

"Caroline, Gretta," I said in greeting. "I don't know if you want to involve yourselves in our Haunting."

"We might need help," Sean said. Maybe we didn't, maybe we did, but I wanted it. Honestly, I was scared of the monster that attacked us. Every time I closed my eyes, memories attacked me of lives slaughtered.

"Actually," Gretta said, "we're due for a Haunting, anyway. That's why we're here. Caroline's losing sleep with worry, so we came by to pick up a prescription. If given the chance, I'd rather join one that's already running and set up with a strong team."

I grimaced, unsure if breaking the rules of Haunting reprieves meant that Hauntings could break the rules around you in return. "We've already lost two. Who knows how many it has killed before we crossed its path?" I couldn't help but wonder about the homeless man and Oz.

"But will you join us?" Sean asked. "This isn't your fight."

"That's right, it ain't their fight!" Blake spat, then gestured at Sean and me. "Working with you two is bad enough! We don't need every man and his dog to come in and take the reward when we kill the thing!"

"I'll vouch for them," I said. "They're fighters, smart and trustworthy."

Ren mumbled something from the corner, but Blake's ranting mowed him over.

"What was that?" I asked Ren.

"A pack might intimidate it," he said. "Werewolves tend to be pack hunters, but this one's a lone-wolf. The larger our pack is, the more intimidated it might be."

I pursed my lips sideways in thought. "So, you're saying we can scare it away with a bigger group? Or would we only enrage it with the challenge?"

Ren shrugged. "Hard to say."

"Either way," Sean said, "the more people we have with us to fight, the better. Caroline and Gretta: you're in. Ren, you seem to know a lot about werewolves. Tell us everything."

Ren shuffled and glanced at Blake as if asking for permission to speak. I grumbled under my breath at his subservience. Why did brains bow to brawn?

Blake made a dramatic show of relenting the attention to Ren. With a deep breath, Ren began, "There are many different types of lycanthropes, or wolf-shifters. The very base definition of lycanthropy is the mental disease of humans thinking they're wolves."

"Ah." Sean nodded. "It's Greek. Lykos means 'wolf,' and anthropos means 'human being.' That makes sense."

I cleared my throat to hide my amusement at Sean's medical interjection. "As fascinating as it is to hear about the origins, can we focus on the type that's trying to kill us? What do you know about it? Characteristics, strengths, weaknesses? It shied away from our bullets, but didn't seem affected. Who shot it at the end?"

Ren shrugged. "I shot it with a silver bullet, but I'm not sure how much damage it actually did. This isn't a human with cannibalistic desires. This is a true shape-shifter."

"Great." Blake grinned devilishly. "So, we can kill it. What are we waiting for? Let's hunt it down and kill it!"

"Oh, shut up, Blake!" I groaned. "Do you even think before you speak? Just because it has a weakness doesn't mean it'll be easy to kill. That means its *only* weakness is silver. Gretta, Caroline. Do either of you have any experiences with werewolves?"

The sisters shook their heads.

Caroline added, "I was nearly bitten by a werehyena when I was three, but it was my parents' Haunting, and I don't remember anything."

Sean's eyes went wide. "Really? That's scary. I've heard stories about Fantasy werewolves that are actually tame."

Ren scoffed. "Werewolves originated in the mountains between Fantasy and Mystery, but Horror strengthens beasts into Hauntings. They lose all sense of humanity when they transform. Even if a Horror werewolf makes it back to Fantasy to weaken their Haunting and use wolfsbane potions, they still crave the hunt."

I blinked, surprised by Ren's knowledge. Hauntings were weaker outside of Horror? That, more than anything else, was a good reason for me to make a goal to emigrate from Horror. Oz would have wanted it.

"Alright," Gretta said, "so how do we fight it? How big is it? What are its strengths? Tell us everything you already know."

I smiled, grateful for Gretta's level-headed directions. Maybe it was good to have her and Caroline beside us for this Haunting.

Blake went into a tirade of hyperboles to describe the werewolf. Sean and I interjected where we could state the facts…as far as we knew them.

"So, its weakness is silver," Caroline said. "Gretta and I each have a pistol and magazine of silver bullets. Unfortunately, we had to sell our silver stakes, but I'd rather not get that close to a werewolf, anyway."

Sean laughed, gracing Caroline with one of his pretty-boy smiles. Wait—what did she do to deserve that smile of his?

"We can set a trap," I said. Why did I suddenly feel the need to prove that I was smarter than Caroline? "We can assume it'll come for Chike and Sean again tonight. Probably Chike, because his deeper wound makes him easier to smell and an easier kill."

"Good idea," Ren said. My insides warmed a little from his acknowledgement, though I wished it had come from Sean.

"What?" Blake asked. "So, we huddle around Chike's hospital room, and as soon as it shows its ugly face—" The rest of his sentence was a collection of explosive sounds.

I scoffed. "Not quite. We need to lure it to a specific area where we can target it without it reaching us. What about the hospital gardens?"

"That should work," Sean agreed, and everything was right again.

Chapter 10

Sean and I each bought an extra clip of silver bullets from various hospital occupants. With no way to verify the legitimacy of their silver, I loaded my three licensed silver bullets after three questionables, leaving the last three questionables as spares.

Our newly formed Haunting group took turns sleeping on the hospital benches while plotting in the lobby.

"So, Chike will be in the center gardens," I said. "Does he know he'll be our bait?"

Blake smirked. "Of course not."

"He should know," I argued. One too many times, I'd been placed as bait simply because my name made people think that I was useless in any tactics. Jerks. I'd been the one to take down the Hauntings when my so-called friends failed me.

Still, a small part of me worried. "The werewolf smelled Sean's blood too," I said. "He could be a target if the Haunting skips over the easy bait of Chike. In fact, that seems more probable. Unlike most hunters, this Haunting didn't seem to target the weak. It went for the strongest first. Sean should be hidden in a defensible position."

Blake scoffed. "Coward."

"It isn't cowardice," I argued. "It's simple survival instincts. Right Sean?"

"You're talking about me?" Sean asked. I was happy to distract him from his conversation with Caroline about the different Hauntings she'd faced and beaten. Show off.

The entrance door opened, and I reached for my revolver. It was only Ren returning from his sleeping break. I released a breath. I was ready for this Haunting to be over. I hated jumping over every little noise and distrusting everyone around me, but that was the way during Hauntings.

No, it didn't need to be.

I turned to Sean, but he'd already returned to his conversation with Caroline. She had his rapt attention over some intense…something. My stomach grew uneasy. Maybe if I stood and walked around, I'd feel better.

I walked over to Ren, who thumbed away on his flip phone.

"Who are you texting?" I asked.

"Huh?" He looked up with a delayed reaction. "Oh, no one. I'm taking notes."

"Oh?" I prodded. "About what?"

"The werewolf we're fighting," he said, thumbing a few more words into his notes.

"You held back in our first meeting," I said. "How much do you really know about werewolves?"

He ducked his head, bashful. "Enough that people make fun of me for it."

"People" probably meant "Blake." I nudged Ren. "Try me."

He hesitated, then said, "I've studied everything there is to know about every kind of lycanthrope. Shooting one was kind of an honor for me."

I smirked. "The knowledge of a mad genius can make you a target. It's dangerous to be brilliant."

His wide eyes met mine. "You think I'm brilliant?"

I shrugged. "I thought my brother was brilliant, but you've taught me things he didn't about werewolves. What else do you know?"

"Really? You want to know more?"

"Yeah." I leaned back and made myself comfortable, expecting a long talk.

"Huh, where to start?" His eyes raced back and forth like he reviewed all his notes before him. "There are so many different kinds. Which one interests you?"

"Uh, just how many are there?"

He grinned. "Just when I think I've learned them all, I learn about a new one. The one currently hunting us, for instance, is something else. I mean, it's obviously not a mai-cob, or a witch in wolf's clothing; or a nahual, which is known for raping and stealing cheese. Those always leave their victims alive."

I gave him a funny look and tried not to laugh about the extremes between stealing cheese and raping.

"At least it's not a Je-rouge," Ren continued. "It doesn't have red eyes and doesn't possess people before transforming. They usually target mothers and ask for children.

"At first I thought it was a loup-garou, which is similar to the wendigo or wechuge, because it's so big. Those types of werewolves grow larger with each meal, but stay thin. But the wendigo is more of a cannibalistic human than a shapeshifter. Our Haunting isn't like that. There are also the vampire-type werewolves."

"Vampire…werewolves?" I asked incredulous.

Ren nodded. "Count Dracula was descended from werewolves, and he could shape-shift at will during the night or high noon."

"Now that's terrifying," I said, growing quiet as my thoughts raced.

Ren continued, "Jonathan Harker even said the count could create fog and control the wild wolves."

"Ours seemed to do that. Is that what we're dealing with?" I asked. "In that case, we should be using tactics against vampires, not werewolves. Wooden stakes, not silver bullets."

"Probably." He shrugged. "It might just be a classic-style. Normal human during the day, delusional monster during the night. It might be a one-hundred percent innocent person without the curse."

I shook my head. "I doubt it. It didn't hunt for meat and blood. It hunted for fun. It was also extra strong. Any normal human couldn't jump that high off a tree without breaking some bones. Also, regular bullets had no impact on it. And it knew that. It was sentient even during its transformation."

Ren's lips drew into a thoughtful line. "It's hard to say. We need more information."

"Unfortunately, we don't have time to research. To learn more about it, we'll need to interact with it, and by that point, we'll be too busy trying to kill it before it kills us."

"We'll kill it," he said, suddenly venomous.

I raised my eyebrows. "You're sure?"

Ren blinked. His lips went thin and eyes went down. "My whole family was killed by a werewolf. That's why I've learned so much about them. I hate them. I want to kill them all."

"Ah," I said, nodding. "My brother always told me that revenge was dangerous and not worth the cost, but I think I'm starting to understand that kind of hate. The werewolf had been lurking around another Haunting victim. Hauntings are typically territorial and don't cross paths, so it's possible this werewolf killed the homeless man in the park...and my brother. If this one is related to my brother's death in any way, I'll happily condemn it."

Ren's eyes met mine, as if truly seeing me for the first time. He gave me a sad half-smile.

I had a strange urge to demonstrate my understanding, confidence, and encouragement in him. Unsure if it was the right move, I rested my hand on his arm. Oz had comforted me that way before, and Sean seemed to appreciate my touch.

"We'll take it down," I said. "Between your knowledge and our strategies, we won't let it take any more lives." I gave his arm a little squeeze, then turned away before I could do anything else potentially awkward. My feet took me back to Sean. Caroline had gone off to take her sleeping break, so I took her spot.

Sean's eyes flickered into a frown as they glanced at Ren. "What were you guys talking about?"

"Hmm?" I asked, my mind distracted by the possibility that I could be fighting the Haunting that killed Oz. "Oh, Ren really knows a lot about werewolves. It's impressive."

Sean pinched his lips inward and mumbled, "More like obsessive."

I heard him, but his sour attitude made me ask, "Huh?"

"Nothing. Did he say anything useful that the rest of us should know?"

I shrugged. "This werewolf doesn't seem to fit a mold. It could be a shape-shifting vampire, needing a wooden stake to the heart to kill it. Also, it could be Oz's killer."

"What?"

"Yeah. Pray that it's not. Because if it is, Blake won't be the only one you'll need to hold back from mad revenge."

Sean grunted. "Let's pray not. Anyway, we discussed positions. I convinced Blake of your marksmanship, so you'll be on level five with Ren on six, and I'll be on three. Hopefully, you'll be safe there." His perfect smile warmed me, and I breathed with relief.

"Thank you. There's a small chance that the Haunting will come after you too, so I'm glad you'll be up there with me." Despite his poor aim.

He nodded and spared me a small smile. "Do you want to walk up the stairs together?"

"Wouldn't you prefer to walk with Caroline?" I asked. I didn't mean to sound snarky, but it came out that way.

He frowned and retorted, "Would you prefer to walk up with Ren?"

"What?" I asked. "No. You're my Haunting partner. You know Oz's rule book, and I've known you longer. I trust you."

His frown lifted into a know-it-all smirk. "Exactly. So why would I want to go with Caroline when she has Gretta to back her up? And I don't want you to go up with Ren. Apparently, I'm the jealous type."

"Huh?"

"Just shut up and take my hand, okay?"

"Um, kay?" I reached for his proffered hand, and we began the hike up four flights of stairs. Even if it was in a tease, he told me to shut up, so I said nothing as we stepped together.

The echoes of our footsteps accompanied our thoughts during the first two floors. Sean's hand started to sweat in mine. He let go to rub it against his pant leg, and bit his lip as he reached for me again.

"I, um, I like this," he said.

"You like what?" I asked.

"Holding your hand."

He swung our hands forward and gestured to our connection with his eyes.

"Oh."

What else would I say? "I like holding your sweaty hand too, even though it sets me off balance while walking upstairs, because if you cause me to fall, at least you'll have a better chance to catch me?" I sensed that wasn't the response he wanted. I didn't know what he wanted. He was acting a little strange, swallowing, sweating, and pressing his lips together more than usual.

"Are you nervous?" I asked.

"I'm sorry," he apologized, releasing my hand again to wipe his against his pants.

"It's okay. We have a werewolf after us, and it smelled your blood," I said. "It's natural to feel nervous."

"No, it's not that—I mean, it is, but…" he flustered.

We reached the top floor and he opened the door for me. This wasn't the first time Sean opened the door for me, but this time he made a bit of a show of it, waiting for me to walk through first.

"Um, thanks?" I said. What was going on? Rather than separating to our positions on opposite sides of the garden opening, I faced Sean and waited for him to spill whatever was distracting him.

"Look," he said, "I know we've called each other our Haunting partners, but this is our first real Haunting together. And…being with you…in the middle of all of this…"

When he didn't continue, I prodded, "Sean?"

He took a deep breath again. "I've been thinking about what might happen if we don't get out of this alive. And I don't want to have any regrets."

"Okay," I said. Whatever was on his mind had him too flustered to concentrate on a Haunting. If listening to him for ten minutes would save his life, then I considered it a small sacrifice. "Do you want to sit?"

A nearby sitting area opened up to the windows of the garden below. Sean nodded and pulled me by the hand to the small couch. I rotated in my seat to face him directly and waited as he attempted to compose himself. He wiped both hands against his pants.

With another swallow, he took a deep breath. His brown eyes met mine as he slowly exhaled.

"Have you ever been in love?"

Chapter 11

I wasn't sure what I expected Sean to say, but I definitely hadn't expected him to ask me if I'd ever been in love. "I'm not sure if I believe in love."

"Oh. Really?" he asked. "But didn't your parents love each other?"

I shrugged. "If that was love, I don't want any part of it. My dad shot my mom during a drunken stupor, then shot himself because of 'love.'"

"Oh." Sean blinked and turned away. Yeah, I was great at these things called relationships.

I flustered, feeling the need to explain. "Like, I get it when you care deeply about someone, that you'd do anything to keep them safe. That's love, right? I shared that kind of love with Oz, but it's not like I ever wanted to kiss him." Unlike Sean. My most secret of dreams imagined Sean's smile against mine.

Sean smirked. "Good. That's gross."

"Kissing my brother, or kissing in general?"

"Kissing your brother," he said, wrinkling his nose despite his heavy blush. "I've heard that kissing the right person can be nice."

Could it be nice? Why did this conversation make my face warm? Why couldn't I stop hoping for this topic to lead somewhere? I wasn't sure where I wanted it to lead, so I played it off with another shrug. "I wouldn't know anything about kissing. I figure love is one of those things like Fantasy magic or Sci-Fian technology. It might work in its homeland, but it doesn't work in Horror."

"Hmm." Sean stared at his shoes. "Well, if it helps at all, I think I'm falling in love with you."

"Wha—"

In the split second that my mind tried to comprehend his words, he leaned over. He pressed his mouth to mine, and I froze.

Sean Chase was kissing me! Was this actually happening?

When I didn't act on my impulse to recoil, Sean took my face in his hands and slid closer.

It was the moment all the fairy tales and Romances dreamed about and spotlighted. They talked about fireworks, flames in their hearts, or chills (which seemed like bad signs to me).

I considered what I should feel as described by the stories. Then, I focused on what I felt. I felt…wet lips.

Sean let go of me, and I breathed with relief. Thankfully, he seemed to think he'd taken my breath away. According to Romances, kisses did that sometimes.

But this wasn't Romance or some fairytale. This was Horror, and this was my reality. If love was real, it existed somewhere else. It happened to other people, but not to me.

Sean's expression tilted with an eyebrow raise and a half nervous smile. "I guess I should have asked first."

"U-um," I stammered. "Maybe. Sorry, I'm kind of new to that."

He pinched his lips together—his lips that so recently pressed against mine. "Was that okay?"

"Uhhh," I slurred. "What do you mean? You want me to rate the kiss?" On what scale? Four stars? One-and-a-half thumbs up? A seven out of ten? I had no other experience for a comparison. It hadn't been unpleasant, but the motion seemed overrated.

"I mean—" he shuffled uneasily "—was it okay that I kissed you? I meant it, and I meant what I said. I've fallen in love with you and have wanted to kiss you for a while now."

I continued to stare at him like a surprised mute. What was I supposed to say? Did he expect something from me? What if I said the wrong thing? I didn't want to disappoint or anger him.

He brushed a flustered hand through his hair. "After everything we've been through together, I can't be just your friend anymore. I care about you too much. If friendship is all you wanted, then…" He paused to take and release a deep breath. "I guess I'd find a way to distance myself. But I can't keep pretending that you don't mean anything to me."

I tried to come up with a response, but my brain was sludge. We couldn't be friends anymore? I'd never had a friend like Sean before, and the thought of losing him scared me.

My instincts confirmed Sean's words. We passed a point of no return. There was no returning to "just friends." We were liabilities to each other now. He would do anything for me, and—I realized—I'd do anything for him. I needed his companionship, his protection, his…friendship that made life worth the fight.

There was no going back with our relationship. Which meant there was only going forward.

I told myself to slow down and breathe. He didn't propose. He only kissed me. That was it. It was just wet lips.

Sean chewed the inside of his cheek and dropped his gaze to my hands. "Won't you say something?"

"Um," I began, my mouth dry, "can my actions speak for me?"

He had only enough time to worry his eyebrows before I smashed my lips to his again. Crap, I had no idea what I was doing. Thankfully, Sean was Romantic enough for the both of us. His lips smiled against mine. For the first time, I *felt* the perfection of his smile. Something in that piece of perfection warmed my core and was beautiful beyond anything I'd ever experienced.

I sagged in his arms and let him decide when to break apart. He continued to smile at me when my eyes opened, encouraging my own smile to rise.

"Are you ready to kill a werewolf now?" I asked.

He laughed. "You're amazing, you know that?"

"I don't really care what I am as long as I'm not dead. Come on."

He relaxed his hold around me, then took my hand to stand together. "You make me want to make promises. Just don't die on me, okay? I think I need you in my life."

I smirked back. "No promises."

Heading to my position, I nearly bumped into Ren.

"Hey," he mumbled at the floor and said no more as he passed us to continue around the hall. Had he seen Sean and me kissing? Probably. My cheeks burned as I thought about him walking in on my awkward attempt to be Romantic. Crap, no wonder he was embarrassed.

Supernaturals, that would only fuel the fire of rumors about us.

But were they true now? At least the part about us being more than friends? Sean said he loved me. Whatever that meant. Supernaturals, the whole thing was too confusing.

Chapter 12

I rubbed my eyes and tried to clear my mind. Focus. Werewolf. Possibly the werewolf that killed Oz. Focus.

I secured my position in the corner of the room and cracked open the window to poke the nozzle of my revolver through. I imagined for a moment that I was a professional sniper, taking down a corrupt tycoon CEO or something from Thriller. The sun would refuse to rise for another four hours. I checked that all six chambers were filled with my licensed and borrowed silver bullets. Another clip of my spare three bullets sat ready in my emergency pack.

I waited with my gun trained on the south-east door that was clearest from my position. If I tried to target all of the doors, I'd miss. Ren took position with his rifle directly across from me on the floor above, aiming at my blind spots. I wanted to give him an encouraging smile, but he refused to look at me. Crap, how awkward had I been with Sean?

Blake left Chike in the middle of the gardens to set up in his own position on the main floor. Chike had a gun of his own, but his hands shook. He did some practice aims, and it quickly became clear that his injured arm was his dominant. He was a sitting duck down there.

My periphery caught movement as Sean shuffled in place to my right, two floors below. He glanced at me and straightened when he noticed me watching him. He flashed me one of his perfect smiles and winked.

Condemnation, he loved me? What did that mean? Apparently, it meant he wanted to kiss me. Considering the lingering tingle on my lips, I wasn't entirely opposed to the idea. I'd wanted to kiss him too, so did that mean I loved him?

Now wasn't the time to sort my emotions. I needed to focus.

Time passed slowly as I waited. Werewolves were fast, and the garden wasn't large. It could probably leap from the doorway straight onto Chike. There wouldn't be time for error. One second might be too late. I had to choose the most likely door and remain focused on it. Any movement in that dark hallway could mean death for Chike.

Wind rustled the leaves below and left curtains swinging in the hospital patient rooms. Someone's door was loose on my floor. I didn't look back to see, but I could hear the slow creak and sudden smack of a door on its frame. The bolt must have been broken as it creaked open again, only to sway on its hinges and smack closed again from the push and pull of drafts.

Focus.

One second would be too late.

I narrowed my sight on the doorway below. Breathe. Slowly. In. Out. In. Out. Out.

That wasn't my own exhale. Someone else breathed near me. The smell of blood and dog wafted over me.

A mangled voice rasped behind me, "You have his scent."

I spun around. Two orange eyes stared at me from the darkness. The Haunting didn't immediately attack me, allowing me to ask, "Who?"

"The hunter who doesn't hunt, one who has survived so many deaths around them. I live to hunt. And my favorite hunt is the careful hunter."

"You killed my brother?" I demanded to know.

"Maybe. He was half dead by the time I got to him. No fun at all. But you…"

Condemnation, what did that mean? If this creature did no more than the final touches, what had really killed Oz? The werewolf stepped closer, moonlight lighting his hideous features as his mouth dropped open and his tongue lolled out. "Oh, yeah. I'm going to enjoy this."

"Pansy!"

"Kill it!"

Sean's shout from his window was quickly followed by Ren's as the quiet boy ran into my room. I turned my gun on the Haunting and fired. I missed as the werewolf accepted Ren's challenge and leaped for him.

"Ren!"

My shout of warning was useless as they scrambled like an egg. Ren couldn't aim his long-nozzle rifle between his attempts to defend himself in the melee. As much as I wanted and needed to shoot the Haunting again, I couldn't track their movements long enough to aim.

Shouts came from below and to my sides, but I didn't dare look away. Ren wrestled in a losing battle against the werewolf that attacked Oz.

Anger built inside me, ready to explode into action. I couldn't stand there. Could I risk shooting?

The werewolf grabbed Ren and slammed him against the wall, dangling his feet above the floor and cracking the wall in several places.

"Ren!"

I aimed for the werewolf's head as it stilled near Ren's neck. *Bang!*

The werewolf twitched. I'd hit it with a poisonous silver bullet, but not in the heart. The shot hadn't been fatal. The Haunting turned its orange eyes on me.

Crap-crap-crap!

I stumbled back and aimed again as the werewolf dropped Ren to the floor and stalked toward me. I aimed in the general direction of the Haunting's chest, then pulled the trigger of my revolver.

The werewolf doubled over on itself. I hurt it!

With a massive lunge, it leaped through my cracked window, shattering it. I fired twice more at its fleeing figure. It jerked once, right before landing on the other side of the garden. How many silver bullets could it take?

More shots and shouts echoed through the garden square. They were incoherent noise to my mind.

Ren.

I fell to my knees beside him. He shuddered.

"Ren! You're alive?"

He trembled with full-body seizures. I holstered my gun and reached for him. He needed to be re-situated. Sean and I hadn't covered seizures in our limited medical studies, but wasn't there something about people choking on tongues? I rolled Ren to his side. All the while, he kept his hand pressed firmly to his neck. Blood oozed between his fingers.

A fleeting thought hoped that it was only a scratch. No. The werewolf had put his face there.

Ren was bitten. He was corrupted.

Chapter 13

Don't be afraid to kill corrupted loved ones, Oz whispered to me.

Crap. Crap-crap-no!

I hated it when my brother was right. Killing Ren would be a mercy. He hated werewolves more than anything. He would hate himself as he became one…as he destroyed more families or spread the disease.

Knowing the truth didn't make the action any easier.

Blinking back tears, I raised my gun again. I thought of the light in his eyes as he talked about mai-cobs and wendigos. Ren's silence sometimes spoke more heavily than Blake's streams of word-vomit. I pushed down the intuition that Ren was a good man with a cruel leader. I forced myself to consider the monster that he would become. His lips pulled back as he snarled into the air.

No. I couldn't let it happen. Not to Ren. Taking him out would be a mercy.

"I'm sorry," I whispered, resting my barrel against his heart.

Bang.

Ren's seizure shuddered to a stop. A spot of red grew on his chest. He jolted as the poisonous bullet spread through him. His eyes raised again to mine. A trembling, weak smile wavered on his lips before he died.

My own lips trembled as my emotions spilled out of me.

"I'm sorry," I cried. "I'm so sorry."

Possibilities died with Ren. He would never avenge his family. He would never graduate from high school. Like far too many citizens of Horror, he would never know the feeling of growing old. He would never experience those things that adults said made life worth living.

I would never know if we could have been real friends.

With that mournful thought, I knew that I would cry over Sean's death.

"Sean!" There would be time to mourn after everyone was safe and that monster was dead. I reloaded my revolver with my last three silver bullets, then ran down the stairs. Screams led my way. I followed the sounds of terror and ran on light feet down the stairwell and through the hospital hallways. Two nurses lay dead in a hallway. Another sat in the fetal position, whimpering to the Supernaturals. Something rattled in a patient's room. With my gun leveled, I stepped through the doorway. A patient lay on their gurney, shaking the way Ren had. Massive puncture wounds curved across her shoulder.

Condemnation. Another bite victim. Swallowing hard, I shot her heart.

Her last breaths replayed through my mind over and over as I stepped from the room. I felt dirty, like I needed a bath with a hard scrubbing from the inside-out. My hands were spot-free, though they felt vile. I wanted to put away my gun and hide it from my eyes, but I still needed it. I needed to focus. The werewolf was still out there, hurting more people. He was the murderer. Not me.

Maybe if I told myself that enough times, I wouldn't have nightmares of these moments. Supposing I ever slept again.

I rounded another corner, swinging my gun and my eyes. A silhouette ran across the hallway. It looked human, but I wasn't sure who it was. I ducked back behind the corner as the monster's shadow gave chase.

One breath…two breaths…

I ran to follow.

The hulking shadow was easy to see, but too fast to catch. I aimed between its shoulder blades and fired one of my silver bullets. The Haunting jerked, though I couldn't tell if it was from injury or surprise. It turned around and flared its bright eyes at me.

The monster roared, and I roared back, "Why won't you die?"

I only had one silver bullet left. It had to be perfect. I took a whole second to aim at its heart and failed to steady my breath as the werewolf came closer-closer-closer.

Ba-bang!

My grip jolted as the sound echoed from an unexpected angle. Sean stood at my seven, revolver smoking. The werewolf's charge cut off with a yip and angry bite as our bullets grazed its ribs.

"Supernaturals, Sean! Warn me next time!"

I rarely missed my mark from only fifty feet, but Sean's surprise blast had jerked off my aim.

Condemnation, fifty feet? It was close and preparing to charge closer.

"Stake it is, then," I said, stashing my revolver and grabbing my silver stake. I didn't have time to eject and reload my gun with useless brass. The werewolf charged again.

"But I—get back!" he shouted. At me or the Haunting? Either way, he kept his eyes on the Haunting and pulled me behind him.

Sean shot twice more, but the Haunting dodged each time. I preferred my revolver and throwing knives because I preferred to fight Hauntings from a distance. Up close, Hauntings were hideous. Orange eyes glowed in the flickering hospital lights. Nostrils flared. Claws curled. Fur spiked with tension. Teeth, sharp like knives and long like children's fingers, dripped with blood. Goopy drool hung from eager lips. My heart both froze from fright and vibrated with adrenaline.

I used the adrenaline to grip the silver stake and prepare my strike.

Sean's gun clicked empty. He swore, then did the dumbest thing.

The werewolf jumped for us, and Sean jumped in front of me.

Fool! I shoved him aside, losing my perfect strike. The werewolf landed on me, digging its claws into my arms, shoving me to the marble floor. My shoulder blades and tail bone smacked hard onto the ground. Rancid breath filled my air, and drool landed on my cheek. Its jaws opened wide around my entire face.

I was close enough to count every one of its poisonous teeth or analyze each flaming particle in its hungry irises.

I didn't. I had other plans while I was pinned under the Haunting's body.

I stabbed my silver stake straight up into its chest. It buckled into itself, but continued to jerk around. Shoving my palm against it for leverage, I yanked my stake back out. Then plunged it in again, a little to its left. The werewolf shuddered. Its eyes met mine as if it meant to haunt me for all my days.

"No," I sneered. "You already killed my brother and last family member. This was my revenge. You don't get one."

Its eyes widened with a final sense of the ultimate end. Then its limbs fell.

Chapter 14

"Pansy!"

Sean scrambled to roll the dead Haunting off of me. "You killed it? Are you hurt? Did it bite you?"

"Just claw-punctures," I said, accepting Sean's help to sit up. "No thanks to you."

"Wha—"

"What the horror was that? You were out of bullets, and I had my stake ready. Why'd you jump in front of me like that?"

"I was trying to protect you."

"You succeeded in being stupid!" I said. I wanted to poke him hard in the chest, but my adrenaline wore off. The pain finally caught up to me, and my hardest poke was a little shove that probably hurt me more than him. "You could have died! What did you think would happen? You'd scare it off with your bravery? It would have clawed right through you! Then, who cares what would have happened to me? I can't lose you!"

Sean blinked. "Is…this your way of saying you love me too?"

"I…" I swallowed. Maybe? "I can't lose you. I can't. Don't ever do anything so stupid again."

He smiled. His big and beautiful grin made me feel warm and soft inside, like sunshine. Or was it just my relief of watching the Haunting bleed out? Sean pulled me into a hug.

"Ow," I complained.

"Oh, sorry. You need a doctor."

"We need to confirm its death first."

"Right."

Reloading Sean's gun, we shot the Haunting with silver in each eye. It didn't heal. With the precision of a doctor, Sean cut open the werewolf to expose its heart. It was gone, shriveled up from the silver poisoning. Only then did I allow myself to collapse into exhaustion. Sometime later (who kept track of time those days?) I was stitched up and laying on a gurney. Sean sat beside me as Gretta huddled with Caroline in her own gurney. Blake wandered over.

"Where is everyone?" he asked. Everyone was there except —

"Chike's dead," Sean said. "While the werewolf went after Pansy and Ren above, an entire pack of common wolves attacked the main floor. There were too many."

"Ren's also dead," I said. "The werewolf bit him. I…"

Sean's hand on my shoulder excused me from finishing that awful sentence.

"I'm so sorry, Pansy." His eyes welled with tears. "I know you cared about him."

I blinked. Sean seemed to take his death harder than I had. Strange Romantic.

"Hauntings require sacrifice," I summarized from my brother's book. "You can't save everyone."

Blake swore and kicked the nearest object within range: a metal chair. It clattered to the floor, sending echoes down the hallways. With a final huff, he asked, "It's over?"

I sighed. "Saying it's over only invites it back."

"But it's dead," Sean confirmed.

"Yes." I didn't dare to say more. Even though the Haunting hadn't been a vampire-werewolf, it wasn't like any other werewolf I'd heard of. Reconsidering Ren's words, how

Dracula had broken off from the original pack of wolves, maybe this one was part of that original pack. The purest, strongest, and most resilient of wolves. That meant it had a family. I hoped we'd be safe from its pack as long as we didn't tempt them.

Blake continued to shout and grab at chairs, as if the tumbling could disguise his cries. The nurses managed to stick him with some sedatives, and soon, he was slumped over the reorganized chairs.

Sean also breathed slowly, allowing himself to relax with the Haunting over. "At least we get the rest of the summer free from Hauntings."

I exhaled, long and slow, drawing in the relief. Yeah, a whole summer with no worries about Hauntings. That did sound nice. So much free time.

Sean reached over to take my hand, and I gathered an idea of how he wanted to spend our summer.

Crap, I had a boyfriend. We finished a Haunting only to start a Romance. What the horror did that entail?

Sure, I found him attractive, both his physical and personality traits, and he supposedly found me likewise attractive. Of my almost eighteen years, I'd never met anyone I liked who actually liked me back. What were the odds that this could happen again? What were the odds of finding the mythical "love" with that person?

Maybe it didn't matter. Sean made me happy. He challenged me to be a better person. We were good for each other. That was good enough for me.

Chapter 15

That summer was actually tolerable at the orphanage. It probably helped that I picked up extra shifts at the hotel to fill my free time.

Too old for the orphanage and too poor without his crony roommates, Blake squatted in a storage unit and decided to hang around Sean and me as an excuse to use the orphanage facilities. A day didn't go by without him attempting to thumb us down, but we put him in his place. Without his friends to impress and back him up, he eventually fell in line.

I did pity him. He'd lost all his friends. I knew how that felt. No, that was a lie. I'd never had that many friends to lose, but I knew how it felt to be alone without backup. So, we allowed him to hover around us. Sean tolerated his presence a little less than I did. Maybe it was because Blake had an uncanny ability to pop in or show up right as Sean's Romantic side started to show. At least once a week, Blake interrupted us before or during a kiss.

Kissing seemed to make Sean happy, and I didn't mind it. Honestly, the motions confused me. What was the point of rubbing our mouths together? A couple of times, I might have felt a stirring within me, but just as easily dismissed it. Maybe those stirrings only came because I expected them.

The school year began again, but this time, we were seniors. Seniors! I had survived to my final year of high school!

While Sean took the wrestling branch of Physical Education, I took cross country. Calculus and Chemistry classes were tough (as expected), but I was surprised to see how often they worked together. My most boring class was Survival 500 (Oz could have taught my teacher a thing or two), and my dumbest class was Historical Literature. Whoever assigned *World War Z* in our curriculum gave no thought to the survivors of Brimstone's recent Mass Zombie outbreak. Sean and I both chose Weapons Training for our elective. Now, if only I could graduate and literally live up to Sean's expectations.

The leaves turned brown then littered the ground. With my eighteenth birthday, I was finally free to leave the orphanage. At least, I preferred to think of it that way rather than the orphanage kicking me out. Caroline and Gretta were kind enough to let me move into their trailer. I scouted the neighborhood before making the move official. With over a hundred trailers, the park had a good variety of sizes and residents. Many were recent "graduates" from the orphanage, like myself. There were a few families and even a couple of retired folks. It was always good to have one of those around for keeping track of local news and gossip.

As we were still in abatement during Halloween, we passed the most dangerous of Horror holidays without incident.

Sean turned eighteen in mid November, and Blake convinced him to move into a trailer together in the same park. They found two more roommates to share their two-bedroom trailer. They weren't the brightest bulbs in the batch, so Sean came over to my trailer a lot. We continued to do our homework together, though Sean's attention span lasted an hour before he would get cuddly with me. We continued to practice at the dojo and review his parents' medical text books during our free time. We even filled out applications to Heartford University Online.

"Why are we doing this now?" I asked. "We aren't even halfway through the school year. How will they know if we live to graduation?"

"We fill out our applications now," Sean explained, "but they won't get back to us until next semester. They have a lot of applications to go through, so they have two eliminations. If our grades and test scores impress them enough now, we'll be accepted. They'll look at our records again later just to make sure we don't flunk. The first time we hear back from them should be mid-February."

"That long?" I moaned. "We've already hit the end of our six-month reprieve. We could be dead by then!"

"My dear Pansy," he said, gracing me with a kiss. "It's only a couple of months away. We'll survive. We'll be accepted. And then, it's only a matter of leaving Horror to attend the school for real."

Despite my worries, I smirked. He really was a dreamer.

During the winter holidays, Caroline faced a snow-Haunting, though she never told me whether it was a mad-man or monster. After the werewolf, the sisters and I mutually agreed not to pull each other into our Hauntings. The less we knew, the less likely we'd become involved.

The winter dragged heavily through January. Snowplows were regular and common enough that we didn't get our first snow day until an unexpected blizzard in February.

Sean cursed, "Dankish, dismal, frost-bitten, spiteful wretch of this weather."

"You're not happy to have an unexpected day off from school?" I asked, confused by his sour mood.

"For some reason, I keep forgetting how depressing the weather is here. In Romance, we'd have a few sunny days by now—bitterly cold, but at least sunny. That blizzard completely foiled my plans. Why is it that whenever we want something to go perfectly, Murphy's Law decides to come into play?"

"What plans?"

He barely seemed to hear me. With his arms folded in thought, he tapped his fingers quickly against his elbow. "The snowplows should clear the roads by this evening, right? Maybe I can still make it work."

"What work?" I nearly shouted.

He finally met my eyes and offered a nervous smile. "Supposing they clear the roads by dinner time, can we go out to dinner tonight?"

I considered any possible problems with his request, then shrugged. "Sure. But why tonight and not another night?"

"Could you wear your green dress? It's a special occasion."

It was? He refused to give me any more details, but kept a secretive smile when reminding me to dress up. I only had a handful of skirts and dresses for church, and my green dress was my fanciest. Sean once called it a "red carpet dress," which confused me with images of bloody carpets. But he'd never asked me to wear anything specific before, so I humored him that evening. Not like it mattered what I wore under my winter coat.

The roads had been salted and plowed enough to travel, letting Sean pick me up at my trailer. He wore a suit and tie. To add to my confusion, he drove me to…the hospital?

Before I could ask, Sean shushed me with another secretive smile, and, "You'll see." He escorted me inside and up the stairs, pausing to quickly reenact our first kiss. He continued to lead me upstairs to the roof with a borrowed key.

I stepped through newly replaced doors and felt transported in time and space. Potted flowers lined a snowplowed path of pink flower petals to a little round table. Dining ware was set for two, lit with candles and a canopy of string lights. Soft violin music played from unseen speakers.

Sean led me to the table and lit the candles while I admired the view from the ten-story building. Between the snow and town lights, it was almost magical. I might have called it breath-taking, except that seemed problematic.

"Is there a funeral?" I asked.

"What?" he laughed.

"You're wearing a suit, and I've never seen so many flowers or candles in one place. Plus, the sad music."

Sean laughed again and kissed my forehead. "No, this is… this is how we date in Romance. We use flowers to express our love, and try to make the area around us welcoming."

"Oh, okay," I said, still a little wary.

"We should probably sit and eat, but…I'm so excited and nervous, I can't wait."

He raised two envelopes.

"Is that—"

"Two letters of acceptance to Heartford University Online? You bet they are!"

"Really? Yes!" I threw my arms around his neck and laughed with joy. I would be the first Finster to receive a college education!

Don't celebrate too early, Oz warned. "Wait, I want to see it."

"Sure, this one's yours. I hope you don't mind that I opened it already. I wanted to know if we'd be celebrating or consoling tonight."

I unfolded the letter and read the words three times to be sure. Yes! I was accepted to Heartford University Online! A dream I never thought possible was coming true!

"Thank you, Sean." I beamed. "I never would have done it without you."

"You don't give yourself enough credit. Besides, this is only the first step. Soon enough, we'll leave Horror and attend in person. Together."

He slipped his arms around me, and his lips smiled before they found mine. I tried to follow his motions, intrigued by the process of learning something new with him. My mouth tingled when he let go.

He replaced the letter in my hand with a pink rose. "Happy Valentine's Day."

"Happy what?" I asked.

"Valentine's Day," Sean repeated. "It's a holiday in Romance, meant for people to express their love for each other."

"Oh," I said, a little embarrassed, and accepted the flower. "Thanks."

I twirled the rose back and forth between my fingers, unsure of what to think. Still reeling from my college acceptance, I felt like an idiot for coming with nothing more than my church dress while Sean made grandiose preparations. I should have known he'd want to celebrate the holidays from his homeland.

Sean watched my twirling and slid a nervous hand through his hair. "I debated whether to get you a pansy flower or a rose, but pansies aren't the easiest flower to gift. I'd normally get a red rose to show my deeper feelings for you, but I know how you don't like red, and I couldn't find one without thorns."

"Sean—" I smirked "—you're rambling. I don't know why you're nervous. This is all very nice. Almost too nice, and I feel like an idiot with nothing to give you."

He reached for me with one trembling hand while his other grappled in his pocket.

My heart stuttered with the possibilities. Why was he so nervous? What was he pulling from his pocket? Had he played me all along to pull a weapon on me now? Not likely, but the reality was just as unbelievable.

"It's okay," he said, pulling a small black box from his pocket. "The only thing I want from you is a 'yes.'"

He dropped to one knee and flipped open the box to reveal a small diamond ring. His nervous smile broadened, and my breath stuttered a little.

"Pansy, I love you. I want to marry you. Will you marry me?"

Supernatural Condemnation. I measured my breathing and told myself to calm down. This wasn't a bad thing. Right? In fact, marriage ensured a Haunting partner. Affairs were sometimes the ugliest Haunting omens, but they were one of the only reasons Hauntings targeted married couples. Sean loved me, and I had absolutely no desire to betray him, so that wouldn't be a problem with us. Even if I wasn't sure if I loved him as much as he loved me, maybe love would grow with time? I had a hard time imagining myself feeling like I did for anyone else.

Besides, Sean hadn't simply given me hope for a better future. He'd made it come true. What more could I ask for in a husband?

"Yeah," I whispered. "Supernaturals, it's mad, but yeah, I'll marry you."

His smile became a full grin, and I stared at his lips like an idiot. There was something about his smile that tugged at me, like a clue to a search I didn't know I was on. My heart leaped within me.

It was maybe only a sample, but it was enough to believe this was a man to protect me, trust me, survive with me…live with me.

Sean covered my mouth again with his own. I kissed him back, elated by the promise that I'd never be alone again.

PART THREE

Chapter 16

This was bad. Sean wanted to wait until after graduation to make our union official. The timing couldn't be worse. We would hit the end of our one-year remission by then, and big events (such as high school graduation and weddings) were like invitations to have a Haunting.

"What are we going to do about Hauntings?" I asked Sean one day at lunch. I was trying hard to be serious between the joyful glances and butterfly stomachs. His adorable smiles and unpredictable kisses were enough to distract all thoughts of reality.

Focus. We had a Haunting coming up.

"What about Hauntings?" He grinned. "We'll fight them together." He took my hand and rubbed his thumb across my skin. Was he trying to soften me up to his opinion? "You'll never fight your Hauntings alone again."

I raised an eyebrow. "That's not a promise, is it? Promises are only broken or—"

"—Kept to an early grave, I know, I know. That's why I didn't say the words 'I promise.'"

I smirked. "I don't think that's what Oz meant."

He squished his lips to the side in thought. "You're right. I'd hate to run into a Haunting during our honeymoon. I mean, I probably have enough from my parents for an exotic get-away to Paranormal or some place, but it's not enough for two of us."

My mind whirled as he spoke. The thought of a honeymoon and all its implications stirred my stomach. Then there was the bit about money from his parents. I never even considered that Sean had an inheritance. He had enough to leave Horror? How rich was he?

Lump sums of money can make motives for murder. We couldn't let anyone know how much money he had.

"So," Sean continued, "is there a way to make sure Hauntings won't come for us during the wedding?"

"Only if we're in remission," I said.

"How do we guarantee remission?"

Blake plopped down beside us. "You search out a Haunting to fight before then, that's how."

"That works?" Sean asked. "We can hunt Hauntings and make them fight us on our own schedule?"

"Nuh-uh." I shook my head. "That's a bad idea. Hunters always die."

Sean pondered aloud, "But Gretta and Caroline joined our fight against the werewolf after their reprieve. They chose to fight the Haunting, survived, and earned another six-month reprieve after."

Blake frowned at me. "Aren't you a hunter? You have all the skills and know-how to be one."

"No," I said. "I've never gone looking for a Haunting. I've tried to avoid them at all costs, but I know that sometimes they're inevitable, so Oz taught me to fight them."

Sean tapped his finger against the table. "Why not look for one? We beat the strongest of werewolves. We could probably face another werewolf and not lose anyone."

"He might have already been on my trail after going after Oz," I said, "and we got lucky."

Blake spoke over me. "Yeah, can you imagine if that werewolf ran into someone else without our skills? Think of how many people we saved because we killed him."

Sean smirked. "If we were in Fantasy, the people would honor us as Heroes."

"Guys," I said, "I'm serious. It's a bad idea. We got lucky with the werewolf. We can't assume any other werewolves would be easier."

Blake shrugged. "Okay, but if a zombie outbreak comes during graduation, or you run into a serial killer during your honeymoon, don't say I didn't warn you."

"He has a point," Sean said with his own pointed gesture. "Hauntings will go after people regardless. I'd actually feel better if they came after us—people who know how to defeat them—than if they went after the helpless."

"People are never completely helpless," I argued. "Or if they are, then it's their own fault."

"Pansy." Sean's eyes met mine. "I want to become a medic so I can help people. What better way to help people than to destroy Hauntings?"

I clenched my teeth to bite back my remarks. Angry people never spoke wisely. And yeah, I was angry that Sean wanted to do something so foolish as to hunt Hauntings.

Instead, I whispered, "Sean, please. I thought we were going to escape to Romance."

He opened his mouth to reply, then closed it again. Blake continued to ramble off the benefits of deciding our own fates. We could guarantee a calm during graduation and our wedding. We could choose our own Haunting, and estimate the severity of it. Sean responded with quiet 'Yeahs' and 'Sures', though I was grateful he took a step back from the Haunting hunting bandwagon. Blake finished his meal first and left with, "Let me know what you guys decide. See ya later."

Sean and I finished our lunches in silence. After swallowing his last bite, Sean turned to me.

"Just once?"

"Once what?" I asked between a mouthful of macaroni and cheese.

"We search out a Haunting just once. Just this one time I'd like to have control of when a Haunting strikes." He took my hand and leaned in to touch his forehead to mine. "Just this one last time. I want to marry you when you're not checking over your shoulder. Let's face one last Haunting together before we run away to Romance."

I swallowed, unsure what to say.

The five-minute lunch bell rang, and Sean stood. "Just think about it."

Chapter 17

Blake slammed a couple of different newspapers on the floor next to where Sean and I were studying. Sean was content to wait until I made a decision about Haunting hunting, and I was content to avoid one as long as possible. Blake, however, pushed the idea every time we talked. I knew we should have studied at my trailer instead of Sean's. The onslaught of newspapers confirmed my suspicions. Regardless of the publication, they all highlighted Dr. Hyde on the front page.

"Look at that," Blake said. "That's a hunter, and that's the kind of honor we'd get for hunting and destroying Hauntings."

"Supposing we survive," I muttered.

Sean reached over to unfold the paper that posted Dr. Hyde's accomplishments on the front and center column. "What did he do?"

"He's a poltergeist specialist. He has exorcized seven malicious spirits in the last seven weeks! Can you imagine? A new Haunting every week! He's a pro! The people he helps even call him a Supernatural!"

"Think of how many people he helped," Sean said. "How many people are alive because a capable survivor stepped in?"

I leaned over Sean's shoulder to read the article, too. I skipped to the end, expecting to find the details of his gruesome death. There was no way his story ended happily. But it did.

The last poltergeist the doctor exorcized was that of Ulysses Dethrage—a tortured soul who killed his girlfriend when he caught her cheating on him. He was killed by her avenging lover, but the idiot died in a car accident before Ulysses could get his own revenge. Left to wander and haunt whoever he wanted, Dr. Hyde was quoted to say, "I need a break after that one."

The article was smart enough not to include the exact sum of the doctor's reward, but the Q&A gave a hint.

Q: What are you going to do with the reward money? Do you plan to return to Sci-Fi?

A: No, those two months of poltergeist hunting was just the beginning. I want to settle down a little to focus on research, because I still have big plans to continue my work. Big plans.

"He's from Sci-Fi," I realized. "Hunting Hauntings earned him enough to return to Sci-Fi. He had enough money to leave Horror."

Sean took my hand and smiled, stuttering my heart. I knew he already had enough money to leave Horror, except only enough for one person, and probably not enough to start a new life. With my work at the Brimstone Hotel, I'd been able to save my reward money from the werewolf. Maybe one more Haunting and a year's worth of work would be enough.

"Okay," I said. "Let's find us a Haunting."

Sean's smile bloomed and my heart skipped again. Blake whooped and began a mad dig through the newspapers.

"There's the anaconda in the nearby river," he said.

Sean shivered. "No. I really don't like snakes."

"Maybe you should face your fear," Blake teased.

Backing Sean, I asked, "Do you know anything about snakes? On a scale of one to ten, how do you feel about a giant snake biting off one of your limbs, drowning you, squeezing the air out of your lungs, and/or swallowing you whole?"

"Okay, fine," Blake grumbled. "Then how about the abandoned house on Ash Lane?"

Sean shivered again.

I palmed my forehead. "I'm regretting my decision already."

"Just this once," Sean reminded me as he flipped another newspaper page. "Hey, look at this. It's a warning to avoid the Forgotten Forest. It says three campers have mysteriously disappeared in the last month. Do you think it's another werewolf?"

"I'd rather not face another werewolf," I moaned.

"Why not?" Blake asked. "They're probably one of the most predictable of Hauntings. Sure, they have some of the most variants, but silver bullets and stakes usually do the trick."

I lifted my head from my hands to analyze the warning closer. "If it's a werewolf, it's the same breed that we faced. It has three separate casualties in the same month, meaning it changes every night instead of the full moon. Oh…"

I drifted as I recognized one of the names of the missing and presumed dead. I hadn't known her well, but she'd been a classmate. Kind and quiet. Could I have helped? Would she have survived if we'd stepped in earlier?

Sean read through the warning again. "It's an unknown Haunting. How many more people do you think will disappear before they even know what kind it is? And if it's a werewolf like the one we fought, how many more people could it kill before someone recognizes its strengths and weaknesses? Someone like us?"

I groaned.

Blake pulled at the paper to have a look. "Sounds interesting. Almost like a Mystery Case. I like it."

"I don't," I said. "What would we do? Go camping and hope it finds us? That breaks all of Oz's rules."

Sean raised an eyebrow. "I thought that was the point. We're breaking your brother's rules to find a Haunting, or to hope a certain Haunting will find us."

I grimaced. "I don't have a good feeling about it."

"I have a great feeling!" Blake grinned. "Let's go during the next holiday weekend. Or are you gonna chicken out, *Pansy*?"

Sean rubbed his thumb across my hand again, taking a more persuasive approach. "Just this once."

I grimaced at Blake and rolled my eyes at Sean. "Fine. But we're only renting camping equipment. I never plan to use it again."

We began a list of the equipment we'd need. Other than our usual replenishments of our emergency packs, we didn't have sleeping bags, cookware, or the first idea of how to acquire such items.

"What about sleeping arrangements?" I asked. "I don't want to sleep in a tent by myself."

"Do we invite another girl?" Sean asked.

"Who?" I asked. "Caroline and Gretta just finished Hauntings last month. They're in abatement, and if they're smart, they'll stay that way."

Sean tapped his fingers on his chair in thought. "Do you want to sleep in a tent with Blake and me? I promise to behave myself."

As if to prove his words, he gave me a quick and innocent peck on my cheek.

"I don't know," I said slowly.

Blake piped up, "I'll sleep between you." The wiggle of his eyebrows wasn't reassuring.

I frowned. "Even though Sean has deeper feelings for me, I trust him to behave more than you."

"Ah," Blake whined, "you're no fun."

"And you're going to get yourself killed," Sean said with a friendly punch. "That's my fiancée you're talking to."

Chapter 18

A teacher-preparation day gave us a three-day weekend in the middle of March and a set time for our Haunting hunting. We spent the days prior researching and shopping for camping gear. We snagged a four-man tent to rent, three sleeping bags, and some hiking equipment, just in case. I stuffed my school backpack with things I hoped to never want and my emergency pack with things I hoped to never need.

We didn't bother renting a car. Vehicles of Haunting hunters would only fail us at pivotal moments, or become damaged beyond repair. We didn't have the money for that kind of insurance. So, we researched long-distance buses. Buses were statistically safer anyway. There were only five other people traveling between Brimstone and Inferno. A half-hour into the woods, we pulled the lever to stop at Boondocks National Park.

We checked in at the park ranger shack, grabbed a detailed map, and were handed a flier of the campground rules. We made a speedy getaway after noticing the park ranger's taxidermy birds in the back of his shack.

Blake grumbled on our way out, "We're in the wilderness. Can't we do whatever we want?"

"Depends on the Haunting you want to face," I said. "Leaving litter around might invite a small Haunting, but starting a forest fire probably invites something deadly. I suspect that the bigger rules we break, the bigger the Haunting will be. I'd rather face a Haunting that comes after us for being so stupid as to camp in the woods while following every rule."

Sean chuckled. "You're so sure a Haunting will come after us. Even if we keep all the rules?"

"I don't know," I said. "Maybe, if we keep all the other rules, this can be a harmless camping trip. Maybe."

Blake stepped onto a large rock on the pathway and jumped off. "But the whole point of this trip is to invite a Haunting so we won't face one later. I'm all for breaking some rules. I can think of one in particular that would be fun."

"Which one?" I asked.

Blake showed off his teeth with a malicious grin. "The number one rule."

I frowned. "You want to break the number one rule to stay away from drugs, sex, and violence?"

He leered at me. "I once heard about a cannibal who only stole away virgins. I'd offer protection."

Sean shoved him back. "If that was the Haunting we hunted, you'd better stay away from her. Besides, I'm a virgin too, so she and I would help each other on that account."

Blake balked. "You admit to being less than a man?"

"He's not 'less than a man,'" I said. "I think it's more manly to have self-control than to take control."

The conversation halted as we reached our designated campsite. The little clearing between the trees was grassy enough for our tent and close enough to a firepit for warmth. It wasn't either abandoned to the whims of the wild or trying too hard to look perfect. Not that I had a lot of camping experience, but it seemed normal, which was oddly reassuring.

With the weather still closer to winter than spring, there were only two other fate-tempting campers occupying the entire site. I thought it best to avoid them if possible. For all we knew, they could be the Hauntings abducting people.

Blake wanted to go swimming in the lake. Without any other ideas, Sean and I joined him on the beach. Blake stripped down to his boxers and did a cannonball off the dock. He emerged from the water with clattering teeth.

Sean laughed. "It's got to be freezing from the snow run-off."

"W-w-whatev-ver," Blake shivered. "I-it's fine. I j-j-just gotta k-keep moving. Y-y-you're just a b-baby."

Sean raised his eyebrow, then raised his shirt.

"Sean—" I started, then stopped at the sight of his torso flexing, stretching, working. Supernaturals, he was a skinned version of the muscles system from his anatomy book. He set his jacket, sweater, and jeans on the log, then grinned at me.

"Are you coming?"

"Horror, no," I said. "I'll grab the towels before you loons freeze your limited brain cells."

Sean laughed, gracing me with a quick kiss on the cheek before hopping into the lake. I kept my ears turned toward them as I rummaged through our packs for our towels, but I was pretty sure the whole valley heard Sean's gasp of "Hoh! That's freezing!"

I returned to the log and placed two towels over Sean's clothes. They were still warm. A strange urge came over me to bury my hands and face into his sweater, inhale his cologne, and —

Yeah, that was weird.

Sitting on a fallen log, watching the boys splash in the water, I realized the appeal to camping. The mountains looked so close, I imagined scaling them in a day. The bright sun glistened across the lake and the air was fresher than a bottle of water. I closed my eyes and felt transported. I could have been anywhere in Novel between the water splashing on the shore, birds chirping in the trees, and my best friend's laughter.

Those idiots were going to give themselves hypothermia.

I scavenged the campgrounds for some kindling and sticks, then struck a match from my emergency pack. The light breeze put out my first attempt, but the second stayed strong. I needed to chop some wood to keep it alive, though.

Sean and Blake joined me on the shore again, teeth clattering, bodies shivering, and muscles…tensed. If I thought Sean looked good before he went in the water, now he was something magnificent.

I handed Blake his towel and wrapped Sean's towel around him with my arms.

"C-c-can we make the f-fire big-g-ger?" Blake asked.

Sean said, "It c-can only b-be as big-g as the pit-t-t."

"How 'b-bout," Blake stuttered, "I th-throw you in the p-pit, th-th-then you'll be w-w-warm."

"Then he'll be dead," I said, glaring him down. "Moving around kept you warm in the lake. Maybe gathering firewood will help."

Sean gave a shaky nod and began searching the area for branches and logs. Blake, however, remained shivering in place. I poked our little fire to keep the embers alive as voices approached.

"Hey, guys," Sean called. "You'll never guess who I ran into!"

Sean walked side by side with a man, both of them carrying an armful of chopped logs. It was the man from the newspapers, Dr. Hyde. The Haunting hunter was a couple of inches shorter than Sean's five feet and ten inches. He wore a camouflage coat with utility pants and heavy boots. Wrapped around his shoulder was an odd gun with a funneled barrel and tank.

"There are three of you?" the doctor asked, his voice a little nasally. "Don't you know these woods are cursed? People are disappearing every week."

"That's why we're here," Blake said. "We're gonna take down that Haunting, and don't you even think about getting in our way."

Dr. Hyde raised his eyebrows, and I quickly added, "Don't mind him. Are you here for the Haunting too? Maybe we could work together."

Blake flustered, but it didn't matter. Dr. Hyde shook his head. "I'm renting a cabin down river a bit. The ranger let me know of the new campers, and asked me to come check on you. Glad I did. That little fire of yours won't keep you warm or safe in these parts. I have extra logs from the winter, and thought I'd share."

"We don't need—"

"Thank you," I said, cutting off Blake. "That's very nice. How do you have time to work with the rangers when you're busy catching ghosts?"

Dr. Hyde shrugged. "Oh, I'm taking a break from poltergeist hunting to work on a project. Helping out the rangers helps me stay in touch with the community. The walks help me clear my head, and—to be honest—it gets lonely out here. If you ever want to stop by for a quick drink or sandwiches, come knock on my door. Just follow the stream, and you'll run right into me."

To be honest? Did that mean he wasn't being honest the rest of the time?

I shook my head. No, it was just an expression. Why would a Haunting hunter lie to us?

He gave us some tips to keep our fire going, then continued on his way to the park ranger shack.

"Now," Blake said, watching him go, "that's a Haunting hunter."

Chapter 19

Blake didn't help Sean and me as we fed the fire. Go figure, he was useless during dinner preparations, too. Sean and I filtered the lake water to add to our MREs and refill our water bottles. As soon as the boys claimed they were dry, they switched out their towels for blankets. It wasn't until the sun started to set that we thought about putting up our tent. Rookie mistake.

We'd never set up the rental before, and frustrations quickly raised as we worked with the dimming sunlight and our headlamps. Of course, our stress only made the situation worse. Blake broke a tent stake by pulling too hard on it, and we didn't have any extras. Technically, we could have used our wooden or silver stakes, but I knew that if we used one to tie down our tent, we'd need it against a vampire or werewolf. Because life was ironic like that.

Sean rubbed his hands over his tired face. "We'll just leave one side less tight. The corners are the important parts, right?"

The sun was well set by the time we finally loaded into the tent, weighing down the loose end of the tent with our packs. We immediately unraveled our sleeping bags to bundle in and arranged ourselves as planned; Blake near the entrance, Sean in the middle, and me on the far end. We had agreed on taking shifts to keep watch through the night, but Blake—who was supposed to take the first shift—fell right to sleep.

As soon as Blake fell asleep, Sean and I found it difficult to join him. His snores rivaled a lumberjack at work.

"How can he sleep with that racket?" I asked.

Sean smirked. "Obviously, he's deaf to himself. If he heard the words that came out of his mouth, I'm sure he'd be nicer."

I smiled back, and Sean's expression softened. He re-situated in his sleeping bag to face me on his side and release an arm above his bag. His eyes shifted to my lips and he leaned closer.

"Um—"

Sean silenced me with a tender kiss. He opened it once before pulling back.

"Yeah?" he whispered.

I swallowed and cleared my throat, wishing it was just as easy to clear my thoughts. "Um, I was going to say we probably shouldn't play with fire."

"We have the fire under control," he murmured, curling his hand around my waist.

"Do we?" I asked, suddenly feeling trapped in my zipped sleeping bag. The best I could do to create space between us was wiggle my whole body closer to the tent wall. "You said you'd behave."

"Pansy, it's just a kiss."

"Yeah," I agreed. "A very nice one that asked for more. I know we're searching for a Haunting and tempting fate in these woods, but we can't break the number one rule."

"What if Blake's right, and the Haunting only takes virgins?"

"Even if some Hauntings target virgins, more Hauntings target infidelity."

Sean fingered my hair in a daze. Did he even hear me?

"Sean?" I pressed.

"Yeah, yeah," he sighed. "It's hard when I love you so much."

Guilt washed over me. Was I only in control of my actions because I wasn't crazy in love? Was I supposed to love Sean to the point of stupidity? That didn't sound right.

I answered Sean by taking his hand. "Get some sleep."

I rolled to my back, relieved as he graced me with a small half-smile. Blake's snores continued to break through the woods like a growling bear, but eventually I fell asleep.

I didn't bother keeping count of how many times I woke in the middle of the night. Despite the grass, the tarp, the tent, my air pad, and my sleeping bag, the ground was hard on my hips. Blake's snores didn't help. More than once, I woke up with one of his snorts, thinking a wild animal was in the tent. By five o'clock, I gave up on sleep. The sun still had a few hours before rising, so I pulled out a book to read with my headlamp. I knew better than to read a Horror history while camping, so I read a tale from Romance.

Earlier that year, I had asked Sean for a good history to understand his homeland, and he suggested *Persuasion*. I had struggled through it. Between the old-fashioned language and ridiculous frivolity, I kept waiting for the vicious and justified deaths of Sir Walter Elliot and Lady Russell.

My current read was Sean's next suggestion, *The Phantom of the Opera*. Their situations were more relatable, but, crap, so much was said with so little done. I read about Christine's abduction by the Angel of Music (AKA the Opera Ghost or Erik) as the day dawned and Sean woke.

"Good morning," he said with squinted eyes and a lopsided smile. He leaned forward as if to kiss me, but I leaned back.

"I have morning breath. You probably do too."

He grunted, then rolled over to grab his hygiene kit. I grabbed my own and decided to face the world again. For all we knew, our tent had transported to somewhere else while we slept.

We weren't even careful as we stepped over Blake, who continued to snore away. We exited our tent to the fresh mountain air. Surprise, surprise. We survived a night in the woods and nothing bad happened. Strange. If we packed up and left, I could tell the unlikely tale of our uneventful camping trip.

But we were supposed to face a Haunting. We needed to face a Haunting now so one wouldn't come after us during graduation or the wedding.

I kept my blanket wrapped around my shoulders as I surveyed our campsite. I didn't know air could smell so clean. Early birds sang from their unseen nests. From the trees to the lake, everything looked so still. It was almost other-worldly with its serenity. Almost…too peaceful.

Then Blake snored and broke the magic.

Sean got the fire going again as I retrieved the frozen breakfast burritos from our cooler, tied up in a tree. I vowed to never complain about standing to walk to the refrigerator again. Blake woke up just as Sean and I finished breakfast, and not a minute earlier. Did I feel guilty for leaving him the most burned breakfast burrito? Nope.

"Alright," Sean said, wiping his hands free of breakfast. "What should we do to hunt a Haunting?"

I shrugged. "Don't ask me. This was your idea."

"Let's break some rules!" Blake said, spitting bits of tortilla and egg.

I frowned. "We already talked about that. No rule-breaking."

"Maybe," Sean offered, "we can go exploring a bit. I brought my mom's old camera to take some pictures."

"Your mom had a camera?" I asked. Oz had always discouraged me from using cameras, because they (like mirrors) usually revealed things you either didn't want to know or could die from knowing.

"Yeah," Sean said. "It's an SLR, so it uses film and everything. My mom used to take lots of pictures, but she stopped when we moved to Horror. Since film's really sensitive to light, you need a room with no light to switch the film in and out. My mom only changed the film once after moving to Horror, and she said it was the most unnerving three minutes of her life. I don't think she took any pictures on this roll of film because she didn't want to use a darkroom again to replace it."

We first explored the lake, walking completely around it. We had to wade across the stream that went down to the rental cabin and accidentally startled some birds from their ground nests. They took off with a sudden rush, and my heart leaped with them. I cried out and tripped into Sean's arms. He laughed and took a belated picture of the birds in flight. He also took a few pictures of me when I wasn't looking. I wouldn't have noticed if the camera didn't have such a loud shutter snap. I studied a possibly poisonous plant, walked with my arms out for balance, or smiled at something he said. Then —

Shh-k!

"Sean!" I complained after he captured me throwing a skipping rock across the lake. "You're supposed to warn people before stealing their souls."

"I'm not stealing your soul," he laughed. "I'm preserving it. Totally harmless."

I stuck my tongue out at him, but quickly pulled it back in when he raised his camera to threaten me with another picture.

We spotted a lone fisherman across the way, but he was gone by the time we reached the other end. Sean and I speculated whether he'd been another camper or some lost spirit of the lake.

We arrived back at our campsite in time for lunch. Again, to my surprise, our things remained untouched. I really thought that if we left it alone, some Haunting would search our belongings. I kept anything of worth in my emergency pack, including *Oz's Haunting Survival Book.*

We attempted to fish with a makeshift stick and string but caught nothing. It probably didn't help that Blake shoved Sean into the water. Sean taught me the basics of how to use his camera, and I caught a few pictures of him in the water, swimming, laughing, looking at me in that special way of his.

That was something I wanted to preserve. The hollow pain in my gut from losing Oz crept open again. If I had a picture of Oz, I would have treasured it. Instead, I only had his words and his voice in my head as I read them.

Sean flicked some water at me, yanking me from my thoughts, and closing that hole again. As long as I had Sean, it was enough.

Chapter 20

I slept better that night. Maybe it was the exhaustion of the day. We'd stayed up into the night, roasting marshmallows over the fire and sharing ghost stories. It was a good way to invite a ghostly Haunting, but the stories we shared were mostly jokes about "black eyed ghosts" and babies with pickle jars.

I woke up to birds chirping and the sound of the lake lapping the shore. It wasn't until I sat up and looked around that I realized the real reason I slept so well.

"Where's Blake?" I asked.

"Hmm?" Sean moaned, eyes still closed.

"Sean, get up. Blake's gone."

Sean blinked awake and breathed in deeply. The cold mountain air bit my skin as I slipped from my blankets. Brrr. Our tent door was open. Blake's jacket and blankets were all still inside. Why would he go out in the cold without them?

Rubbing my hands up and down my arms, I stepped from our tent. Blake was nowhere to be seen.

"Blake?" I called. No answer. I cupped my hands around my mouth and shouted again. "Blake?"

No answer.

"Blaaake!"

Sean crawled from the tent and fumbled to his feet.

"It's freezing out here. Maybe he just went to get some firewood."

"Without our hatchet?" I asked.

Sean shrugged. "Maybe he went to steal some from Dr. Hyde. That sounds like Blake."

That did sound like something Blake would do. It was rude, selfish, and reckless.

"Then we should go after him," I said.

Sean nodded. We took only enough time to put on proper shoes, jackets, and our emergency packs.

Sean pointed the way. "He said his cabin's just down river. The campgrounds extend for another mile, so he'll be a bit farther than that."

"Right."

We set off at a light jog. As much as I wanted to run after that idiot, there was no pathway along the river, forcing us to watch our step over the uneven ground and rocks. It took us longer than expected to reach the national park border. We easily swung our legs over the chain-link fence, then shivered.

"Is it just me," Sean asked, "or is the air colder on this side of the fence?"

"It's colder," I said, shivering again. Hopping the fence was crossing a threshold of security. Even if there was a Haunting somewhere in the park, how many more were in these un-claimed woods?

Sean took a couple of careful steps, but I remained. "I don't like this, Sean. I feel like we're being watched."

Sean stood still save for his head shifting at the slightest noise. A faint breeze tickled my ears. Trees rustled like they whispered to each other.

"Sean?"

He only responded with more little head shifts.

"Come on, let's go back," I said. "Maybe Blake didn't come this way. He could have gone anywhere. Maybe he went somewhere to pee, and now he's wondering where we are."

"Yeah." Sean finally took a step back to me. "Yeah, you're probably right. Let's get back to our campsite."

We jumped back over the fence with little care for our landing, then dashed back in silence. As Sean said nothing, my mind created its own theories. I prayed to the Supernaturals that Blake waited for us back at the tent. Sure, we came out here looking for a Haunting, but worries still clenched my heart about actually running into one.

Our campsite was empty. I shouted Blake's name and Sean checked the tent. No Blake. We grabbed some quick granola bars to feed our anxious energy, then went to the park ranger shack.

"We need to report a missing person."

The ranger simply pointed to the papers on the counter. "Fill those out. You should probably pack up and leave before nightfall."

I frowned. "You don't seem surprised that we're here to report our missing friend."

The ranger sighed. "I warned you when you got here that people have gone missing from this park. Then, you've been shouting someone's name all over the lake. I'd say it's pretty obvious. One of the other campers complained about your racket. They've packed up and left for a quieter scene. Don't get your hopes up of finding your friend. If you stay here any longer, you'll just end up missing, too."

I crossed my arms and studied the ranger as Sean filled out the papers. As soon as we returned to our campsite, I pulled Sean to the clearing. If anyone wanted to spy on us, they'd need to do it in the open.

"I don't think we can trust the ranger," I said.

"What? Why? What about the camper who left? They could have taken Blake with them."

I shook my head. "Hauntings are usually territorial and stick to one area. And if people have gone missing, why hasn't the *park ranger* gone missing? Also, he knew Blake was missing."

Sean's eyes widened. "You think he's the Haunting?"

"Maybe. You saw his taxidermy collection in the back? If he likes stuffing birds, who knows what other animals—or people—he's stuffed."

Sean wrinkled his nose. "That's disgusting."

"It's a possibility."

"But why would anyone want to stuff Blake? Wouldn't you be in more danger, pretty as you are?"

I rolled my eyes. "It's probably just because Blake was closest to the tent door. He was the easiest to reach."

"In that case," Sean said, "we should sleep with our feet on the door side tonight."

"You want to stay here, even after the ranger's warning?"

"I don't like the idea of abandoning Blake," he said. "Even if it's too late to save him, I want to know what happened to him. Besides, who's to say the Haunting will leave us alone if we try to run away?"

"Good point."

Sean and I spent the afternoon and evening loitering around our campsite. As much of a pain as Blake was, his disappearance put a somber mood on us. We quietly discussed different methods to confirm the ranger's Haunting status, then how to possibly end him. While eating dinner, we made a bold plan that involved someone distracting the ranger while the other searched his office. We cuddled closer in the firelight as the sun disappeared behind the tree-line. Little was said as we rearranged our bedding to put our feet toward the door, then shimmied into our sleeping bags. Sean agreed to take the first night watch, then wake me to let me take the morning watch.

I couldn't stand the thought of either of us disappearing in the middle of the night. If we could keep contact in our sleep, then we'd be alerted if one of us was taken.

"Sean," I peeped, unsure how to voice my need, "will you…hold me tonight?"

His face slowly turned toward me. Then, with the same bewildered slowness, he blinked.

"Nothing salacious," I said. "Simply hold me so I know you're here, and I know that *you'll* know I'm here."

He wiggled closer to me and slid his hand down my arm until our fingers interlocked. "Pansy," he whispered, "my dear Pansy, yes."

We lay side by side, holding hands. The windy night brought a chill with it, and I shuffled closer so our arms lined. Sean rolled to his side and extended his arm to brace my head like a pillow. Then I curled into him. His other arm draped over my waist and held me close. He was so warm. And I felt… safer there. Safe enough to drift to sleep.

Chapter 21

I woke up cold.

Why was my sleeping bag completely open? Why was my blanket spread so wide? Why was —

Why was I alone?

I sat up as the chilly air sank to my bones.

"Sean?"

The tent door was open again, revealing the faint morning light. He hadn't woken me for the morning watch.

"Sean?" I called again, a little louder. Raising my blanket around my shoulders, I peeked out the door. Our fire was dead. The campsite was empty.

No. Not again. Not Sean.

Socks, shoes, jacket, then I was out. My three-sixty scan revealed nothing new. Everything was deathly still. Not even a breeze rippled the lake or trembled the tree branches.

"Sean!" I hollered. No birds rustled from my disturbance.

Oh, Supernaturals.

My situation couldn't get worse. I was alone in the woods. There were two things I could do to fix it: not be alone, or not be in the woods. My initial instinct said to run. Run away from these condemned woods. Run away while I still could. But then I'd leave Sean behind.

Even if I managed to escape these trees, then what? I would still be alone. The ache in my chest came back and I made up my mind. Find Sean. Then escape together.

To find Sean, I needed to find and fight the Haunting. To find and fight the Haunting, I needed help. I couldn't trust the park ranger. There was only one other camper in these forsaken woods—another stranger and suspect of abducting my friends.

I stalked to the other campsite, darting between the trees and crouching around shrubs. I hated going slowly when Sean was missing, but I wouldn't do either of us any favors by acting brashly. I knew nothing about our Haunting other than its tendency to abduct people in the woods. To fight it properly, I needed to know more about it.

Even if the unknown camper wasn't the Haunting, maybe they knew something or could help me.

Checking my surroundings before making any movements, I eventually made my way over to the other campsite. The lack of movement and sound confirmed it as vacant. I tiptoed up to a gray truck parked beside a green tent pitched with tight strings. A canoe was strapped to the truck and fishing rods rested in the bed. Was this the fisherman we spotted?

I examined the truck and tent for anything large enough to hide a body, but found nothing suspicious. That wasn't enough to let me lower my guard, especially as a frustrated voice cursed nearby. I dashed away to a hiding spot that let me watch the campsite. With another curse, I found the frustrated fisherman standing in the next empty campsite, holding a flip phone high in the air.

Creeping closer, I managed to overhear his mutters, "Come on, where did it go? Ah—yes! There it is—a bar!"

Standing still at an awkward angle to keep the signal, he made a call.

"Hey, Honey," he said with a warm and kindly voice. "Looks like I found a spot with reception… I know, I miss you, too. I'll be heading home today. I haven't caught anything, but this place is giving me the creeps. The rumors about people disappearing from these woods seem to be true, and I feel like I'm being watched."

He paused to look around himself, and I ducked deeper into my hiding place.

Continuing his phone call, he said, "There seems to be some high school dropouts enjoying an early summer. I worry about Ellie growing into a troublemaker like them."

I almost laughed. I'd never been called a troublemaker before.

"You're right. I'll aim to be home before nightfall. I love you." He hung up and headed toward his campsite. I watched and waited as he began packing his gear.

Was he genuine then? Could I ask him to help me find my friends? Maybe he'd think we deserved it for being "trouble-makers." Besides, if the man was honest, then he had a family to care for. Also, he wasn't my only option for help. There was someone else just outside the campgrounds. Lucky for me, he was a renowned Haunting hunter.

Spying on the other camper had taken my whole morning. With the sun high overhead, I returned to my own campsite, famished and anxious.

After a quick and hearty lunch, I geared myself the best I could to exit the safety bubble of the park boundaries. That included dressing for a high-adventure hike with proper shoes, all my gear in my backpack, and, of course, my emergency pack. The last thing I wanted to do was wander through Haunting territory alone, but what other choice did I have?

Keeping an eye out for the park ranger, I stalked through the camp. Normally, I considered myself light-footed, but there was no quiet way to walk over the rocky path. Though it was dangerous to leave the path, I planned to do a lot more than that at the fence. I made my way through the fauna, careful with each step to avoid crushing twigs and brushing ferns. Unfortunately, that doubled the time it took to reach the edge of the camping grounds a mile away.

The fence was a welcome sight. Even if the park ranger caught me now, I doubted he would chase me beyond the park boundaries.

Hopping the fence, the same chill waved over me as the day before. Gritting my teeth, I pushed onward. There was no other option.

I followed close to the stream, allowing its bubbling to mask my noises. Dr. Hyde underestimated how close he lived. I walked until the sun touched the tops of the nearby mountains. I ate a granola bar while walking, but by 5:00PM, I needed to rest.

I allowed myself enough time to rest against a tree that didn't look too suspicious. I still checked my back or above me in the branches every few seconds for bugs or snakes. I emptied my water bottle down my throat, then used a filter to refill it from the stream. I tasted it first. The water was incredibly chilled, though I didn't know if it was from the mountain run-off or from the extra cold air in this area.

As long as it didn't kill me.

I continued, praying to the Supernaturals that this wasn't a false lead, that this stream really did take me to the Haunting hunter, and not some crazy lunatic in the woods.

A twig snapped behind my tree.

I jumped and turned around. No one was there.

My dagger was in my hand within seconds. I saw no one, but birds suddenly took flight a couple of trees away.

Trust the instincts of animals.

I ran.

If running through the park foliage was tricky, running through the wild woods was down-right hazardous. And I did it with a blade in my hands. Not that I was about to give up my dagger any time soon. As long as those bushes rustled behind me, as long as that breeze whispered inaudible words, as long as my two feet could carry me, I would run.

More twigs snapped behind me. Bushes swished angrily in motion. The breeze grew louder until it huffed in my ears like someone's breath.

I spun around, armed with my dagger, to challenge whatever chased me. No one was there. The air rushed past me, almost with a chuckle.

Shaking, I grabbed my revolver from my pack to have a ranged weapon. But if my enemy was incorporeal, I wasn't sure how useful bullets would be.

I turned back to continue downstream and spotted the rental cabin. It called to me with lights that shone from its windows.

Thank the Supernaturals.

The cabin was a piece of perfection in the middle of insanity. A little white picket fence surrounded a green lawn, well-watered with the first signs of spring growth. On the corner of the lot stood a little shack that hummed with water pressure and electricity. Dead ivy crawled up one side of the wooden cabin, and smoke rose from its brick chimney.

I bounded over the fence, ran up the porch, and pounded on the front door.

"Dr. Hyde? Hello? Please, I need your help!"

Chapter 22

The door opened and my fist almost hit the man inside. Dr. Hyde stared at me in surprise. He wore flannel pants and a plain t-shirt under a white lab coat.

"Who are you?" he asked.

"My name's Pansy," I said. "We met the other day at the campgrounds. I was with two other guys. They're now missing, and I need your help to find them."

He stared at me for a long second, then blinked. Wasn't he supposed to be smart? He had to help me, right? "Please, help me," I repeated. "I think the park ranger is in on it. There was no one else I could go to."

Stares. Blink. Please, please, please?

"Of course," he said, stepping aside to welcome me into his temporary home. "Come on in. Do you need a drink? You can tell me more as I put something together."

I wanted to shout that there wasn't time for idle chitchat, but I didn't have a solid plan to rescue Sean. I didn't even know where he was.

I stepped into Dr. Hyde's cabin, and he went to the kitchen. The cabin was a simple home. The main room included the family room, dining room, and kitchen. All the furniture was simple and old. A couch faced a coffee table and fireplace, and the small dining table only had one chair. Every surface was half covered with papers and notes.

"Ignore the mess," he said, flustering with the papers. "I wasn't expecting company."

"It's okay," I said. "Are those for your new project?"

He turned to me, surprised.

I shrugged. "The newspapers said you're taking a break from Haunting hunting to work on a project. Is it something that can help me find my friends?"

He snapped out of his surprise a belated second later. "Maybe. Not likely, but I really think I'm on to something. I just need the right—I'm so close. I can feel it."

He shuffled his papers together from the tables and counters, then went to one of the doors. "One second. Let me put these away, then I'll get you that drink."

"Sure," I said. What was he working on? A new weapon? A strategy to fight Hauntings? He closed the door behind himself, then I heard the wooden creaks of footsteps on stairs. I listened for footsteps above, but didn't hear any. A basement then? Interesting. Basements and attics were usually not good places.

Only then did I realize that I still held onto my knife and revolver.

Crap, no wonder Dr. Hyde was weary of me. I'd shown up at his doorstep alone, ragged, and armed. I stored my weapons in my emergency pack while admiring the weapons available around me. There was a rifle in a glass case and a line of kitchen knives that hung above the stove on a metallic bar. Could we use those against the park ranger?

I went to his sink, debating whether to top off my water bottle, when footsteps came back up the stairs.

Dr. Hyde returned from his basement. A muted thudding echoed in my ears until the scientist shut and locked the basement door. "So, what can I do for you?"

I cleared my throat. "Dr. Hyde, I've read about your successes with Hauntings lately, and hoped you could help me find my friends. I think the park ranger is a Haunting, or helping a Haunting to abduct people from the park."

"The park ranger?" he asked. "You think he's a Haunting?"

"Or helping a Haunting," I clarified. "People have gone missing from the park before, and the park ranger hasn't done anything about it, and he's the only person there who's unaffected."

Other than Dr. Hyde… I shivered at the thought and tried to push it away. It remained.

How did he live out here all by himself in these creepy woods? The wind moaned around the cabin, almost like it was in pain. Or was it moaning from below? What was that quiet thudding that vibrated the floor? The single chair at the dining table stated his solitude, but if he lived alone, then who (or *what*) was in the basement?

The doctor spoke about the possibilities of a monstrous Haunting, like a siren in the lake, or werewolves in the woods.

No, Blake and Sean played in the lake without any issues. And our tent door was zipped open—not ripped. The more I thought about it, the more I was sure; the Haunting was intelligent and careful. That meant it was likely humanoid. And that narrowed my options to the park ranger…or Dr. Hyde.

Condemnation, had I just walked into the spider's web? Despite the fireplace and closed windows, I shivered.

I couldn't let him know that I suspected him. Another plan formed.

"Maybe you're right," I said. "It took me a few hours to sneak out to your cabin, but I'll probably need to run back to reach my campsite before dark. Can I count on your help tomorrow?"

Dr. Hyde frowned. "Your friends have disappeared each night. You might be next."

"I know, but…maybe I'll leave the campgrounds. I need to leave. Excuse me."

I grabbed for his front door, then bolted out. With the Supernaturals' favor, he had another slow moment to realize what happened. I ran down the porch and around the cabin. I barely made it to the utilities shack before the front door opened again. Ducking behind the walls, I spied for Dr. Hyde. He stared into the woods, looking for me. He bounced something in his hand that gleamed from the cabin lights. What was that?

Either he was a good man who wanted to ensure my safe return to the campgrounds, or a Haunting who thought I knew too much.

Then, he did something I hadn't expected. He clenched the shiny item in his hand, then slammed it into his chest.

He stabbed himself? No, he held the item there and slowly pushed it in farther. A syringe?

That couldn't be good. My bets leaned toward Haunting influences.

The doctor shook with tension, quivered, then yelled into the night. He withdrew the syringe, then smashed it to his porch.

Still trembling, he stepped off his porch and off his property. Then he ran. I waited to lose sight and sound of him before creeping away from my hiding place. I ran back to the house. The front door was unlocked, but the door leading to the basement wasn't. Using my dagger's pummel, I smacked at the lock until it broke.

Behind the door was a dark and descending stairway. I crept down the stairs, measuring the weight on my feet to make sure each step held me before I trusted it. The air was stale and dusty. Why did the door look frequently used if everything down here was coated in dust?

No, not everything. A wedged clearing of the dusty floor revealed a certain shelf that pivoted like a door on multiple occasions. I pulled on the shelf. The wall behind it broke free, bursting with white light.

Dr. Hyde had a laboratory in his basement. Thuds and muffled wails became clearer. Going inside would break at least three of my brother's rules, but if there was a slim chance of finding Sean or Blake inside, I had to check.

Gritting my teeth, I stepped into the white light.

Chapter 23

I walked through a little hallway between four different rooms. Cells actually. The first prisoner writhed on the floor, scratching himself raw. Rashes showed where he wasn't covered with bandages. In the next room, a woman sat curled in the fetal position, screaming at the voices in her head. The thuds came from the third cell as a young woman threw herself at her door. Was that my classmate who had been abducted from these woods? I barely recognized her behind her bruises and crazed expression.

The final cell confused me the most. A person *flew* in crazed circles as the entire mattress, bedding and pee-pot flew around the room in a whirling vortex. The person didn't fly with the regular motions of a caged bat. The body flopped around, completely limp.

Then, I saw his face. Blake.

I gasped and stepped away from the cell. His face was sunken and slack. Whatever Dr. Hyde had done to Blake, it had killed him. My initial desire was to free them. But no, they weren't human anymore. I analyzed each of the prisoners—no, test experiments—again. If they had one commonality, it was that they all acted possessed.

Condemnation.

Needing confirmation, I stepped beyond the hallway of cells to the main laboratory, where another prisoner was strapped on a gurney.

Sean!

Passing cabinets of testing fluids and stacks of papers, I ran to his side. He was connected to more than a dozen tubes and IVs.

"Supernaturals, what did he do to you?" I shook his shoulder, praying he was still alive. "Sean!"

He winced and moaned with pain. His face squished as he tried to open his eyes. His gaze found me with a sliver of a squint.

"Pansy? You came for me?"

"Of course. Let's get out of here." I pinched off his tubes and tried to leave as little evidence of my presence. Who was I kidding? Even if the doctor Haunting didn't know I was here, he would seek Sean and me because we knew too much. I helped Sean to sit up.

He moaned with a hand to his forehead. "How did you find me?"

"We're in a basement laboratory in Dr. Hyde's rental cabin, a few miles from our campsite." I detailed the rest of the grounds as Sean slowly woke. "Do you know if he did anything to you?"

"I feel tired, but I think he only injected me with prep work. I don't think I'm like them yet." He nodded toward the rooms of possessed people.

"Do you know what he did to them?"

Sean snarled. "Yeah, Dr. Hyde talks a lot. He spent some time in Sci-Fi and got this crazy idea to inject people with poltergeists to give them kinetic powers. Crazy, right? There's no way it'll work without killing the person's sanity."

"Supernaturals," I cursed. "Yeah, I don't think you'd be as functional as you are if he'd experimented on you. Let's get out of here before he comes back. Any ideas on Dr. Hyde's weakness?"

Sean nodded. "He's insane, but he's human. If he shows any kinetic powers, we can assume he has the same weaknesses as any poltergeist. That's water, right?"

Water. I pulled out my half-empty water bottle. There was the stream off the property, or the sink upstairs. There was no form of water in the laboratory. Where did Dr. Hyde wash his hands? How many health violations did he break for his make-shift surgery room?

"We can't fight him in here then," I said. "We need to get upstairs or back to the stream."

"What about outside?" Sean asked. "I bet there are tools in the shed."

"Come to think of it…" I laid out a plan to fight the doctor, then a back-up plan if we needed to fight a poltergeist.

"It's insane," Sean said, rolling his shoulders back, "but I think it'll work."

"What will work?" a voice asked from the room entry. My blood froze.

Dr. Hyde stood at the doorway of his laboratory. He slowly lifted his arm and reached toward us. The doctor's smile and every tool started to quiver and rise.

Supernaturally Condemned Crap from Horror!

Time slowed as my mind analyzed every terrible part of our situation. The plans that Sean and I discussed were placed outside, in his yard, or in the woods. There were no windows to escape. There was only the secret door down the hallway of cells, blocked by Dr. Hyde. We were trapped. We were also surrounded as incision tools rose from every direction. Even the notepapers that Dr. Hyde brought down earlier fluttered up like a tornado of future paper-cuts.

We were surrounded by a single man who was infused with a poltergeist.

"Look at this power!" he said. "And I do this with the safest of the poltergeists I caught. I saved the strongest for last, you know? The powers of Ulysses Dethrage are yours for the taking!"

Sean spat like the doctor's words left an unpleasant taste. "That's crazy. Evil doesn't share power."

The doctor laughed. "Exactly! But I do! We're on the same side!"

As the crazy doctor spoke, I felt through my pack for my recently pocketed revolver. "Never!" I shouted back, drawing up my gun and aiming at the Haunting. "You're insane!"

He was a scientist on the brink of discovery, harvesting poltergeists to give humans kinetic powers.

The doctor sighed. "If you don't want to join me, then I believe the term for scientists…is 'mad.'"

Syringes, clamps, scalpels, and scissors raced toward us.

I fired.

A little yelp echoed the bang of my gunshot. It didn't matter if a wall of papers flew around us. My aim was true.

He crumbled to the ground, and every flying instrument followed him to the floor. Blood soaked through the doctor's chest.

"Let's go!" I said, pulling Sean to the exit. Before we came within arm's reach, I fired again at the doctor. This time in his skull. A dirty feeling rose in my gut as I purposefully fired my weapon at a human being. Sean and I ran past the cells of possessed people and through the hideaway door. I turned around to close it behind us, catching a glimpse of papers lifting from the floor.

No, Dr. Hyde wasn't human. He was a Haunting like the deranged souls in the cells. The poltergeists lived even within Blake's dead physical body. We weren't free yet.

"Go!" I shouted to Sean, pushing him up the stairs. We needed to kill a poltergeist next. That meant we needed to get to water. We barely made it up the stairs as the hideaway door was thrown open. Scalpels buried themselves into the stairs, and clamps smacked against the door behind us.

Sean threw me one of his dashing smiles as we scrambled from Dr. Hyde's whirlwind of incision tools. I couldn't help but smile back, relieved and grateful to have him beside me in this fight. We'd come looking for a Haunting, and one found us. The odds were against us, but Sean gave me hope.

The insane scientist levitated up the stairs, raising every hand-sized object in the main room with a raise of his arms.

We scurried into the kitchen and ducked behind the counter extension. It was a terrible hiding place, but worked as a barricade from the foray of knives. A fire poker sailed over our heads and skewered a painting across the room.

Drawers sprang open and every sharp utensil, from cleavers to butter knives, flew through windows and cupboards. Sean and I crouched low as the kitchen shredded itself.

"Pansy?" Sean's grin faltered with unease.

"Shh, almost there," I said. The knives landed dangerously close, though a knife in the *room* was dangerously close. I nodded to Sean, and he chucked a metal spoon beneath the table to send a clatter in that direction. Dr. Hyde flung a knife at the table, and I used the distraction to swing the last drops of my water bottle over our island barricade.

A small sizzle and screech confirmed that my water struck the poltergeist-infused doctor. In his moment of weakness, we bolted for the back door. The stupid lock was jammed. We weren't the type to waste time and shout "hurry!" as one of us struggled to finagle the lock. Sean and I kicked at the glass door together. My ankle twisted with the imbalanced collision as the glass shattered. We tumbled through and stumbled back to our feet. A paring knife and three butter knives hovered in the air between the doctor and us. Their points marked us.

Sean and I dashed into the backyard. My ankle pricked painfully, and I ran a step behind. We couldn't hide with our footprints in the frosted spring grass, and we couldn't run fast enough to escape. We tried anyway.

We sprinted for the utility shed across the yard. Halfway there, a sharp pain zipped up my leg. I screamed and fell forward. A paring knife stuck into the back of my knee. Blood streamed down my calf.

Sean turned his eyes back to me, terrified.

"Keep…the plan!" I shouted through tears of pain. Supernaturals! It stung!

Sean stepped toward me, but I couldn't let him die with me.

"Run!" I shouted.

His eyes showed the conflict, hesitation, and then bitter conclusion of his thoughts. He obeyed me and ran for the shed, leaving me to the fate of the doctor's knives.

I rolled to my back with my good leg. The doctor levitated above the lawn. Three butter knives hovered over me and slowly turned down. They would impale me. I pictured my pathetic obituary; "Death by butter knife, in the middle of a fresh lawn."

I survived sadist foster parents, a masked murderer, and a werewolf hunt to die like this?

The knives fell, and I shouted, "Now Sean!"

My vision became a white fan of mist. Even my hearing became muffled behind a steady "shhhhh." Above all else was an inhuman scream.

Sean had turned on the sprinklers.

Dr. Hyde's lust to kill me kept him distracted as little sprinkler heads popped out of the ground for the first time since winter. With the powers of a poltergeist, he also had the weaknesses. The knives fell with simple gravity, and I rolled out of their way. Their master screeched like a car slamming on its breaks into a murder of crows: a sound of victory.

Chapter 24

I called out to my fiancé, needing confirmation that he was alive and well. Sean stepped out of the tool shed to hear me better and witness the doctor sizzle. I slowly crawled toward the shed as Sean confirmed the doctor's death, then turned off the sprinklers. "Did we get him?"

"I think so," I said, reaching the shed and reaching for Sean to help me stand. I didn't dare to say more since the words "I'm glad that's over" were an invitation to bring it back.

Sean pulled me into a hug of relief. But my brother's words haunted me.

"Remember," I said, "don't celebrate too early. We're not out of the woods yet."

Sean leaned back and smirked. "Figuratively and literally."

I nodded. We needed to return to the campsite to call the Haunting Investigations Unit.

Despite Sean's lethargy, he wrapped my arm around his shoulders to help me limp back to the campgrounds. The park ranger's shack was empty when we arrived, but we found the ranger…rifling through our tent and belongings.

"Hey!" Sean shouted.

The ranger literally jumped and stared at us like we were two ghosts who'd said, "Boo."

"You're back? S-sorry, after so many disappearances, I thought you were goners."

"You'd better return anything you took," Sean threatened. "Either way, we need to call the HIU. Dr. Hyde is dead, and you won't repossess—" His voice faltered as he realized a double meaning to his last word.

"Sean?" I asked.

He shuddered and shook away the recent trauma. "You won't be taking any more belongings of disappeared campers."

The park ranger narrowed his eyes and began to lift a corner of his lip.

Sure, I leaned against Sean for support against my stab wound, but that didn't slow my speed for snapping out my revolver and aiming at the ranger's face.

"Call the HIU," I said, "or else. I am so done with this camping trip."

The Hauntings Investigation Unit showed up like a SWAT team. They flooded the campground and asked Sean, me, and even the park ranger a million questions as the paramedics tested Sean and me. As interested as I was in the paramedics, I was too exhausted to care about their work, other than their diagnosis of Sean.

"He should be okay," one said. "He's had a few recent injections, but based on his vitals and responses, we think they were only sedatives. Right now, he just needs some rest."

My own first aid was simple enough. I had a couple of nasty cuts on my forehead and behind my knee that the paramedics struggled to bandage. Showering would be an issue.

Unfortunately, they said there was nothing they could do for the four experiments in Dr. Hyde's basement. I'd already known Blake was lost (I couldn't remove the image from my brain of him limply flying around), but I lost hope for the others as they screamed at the voices in their heads. The HIU set the entire rental cabin on fire, sending the souls with prayers to the Supernaturals for mercy.

Sean and I returned to our homes, exhausted, but relieved. The rest of the year was a breeze in comparison. Sure, there were school tests, but we didn't fail.

Sean and I attended our graduation ceremony, then quickly left. Turned out, that had been the right choice. One of Sean's roommates had invited a demon Haunting to the after-party.

Instead, we had our own little ceremony with a court judge, a rented dress and tux, and two rings. Sean had griped during our wedding plans, wanting to make a huge spectacle about the ceremony that would have surely invited a Haunting or two. I eventually convinced him that with Horror weddings, the smaller, the better. We compromised with a promise to eventually renew our vows in Romance.

For our first night after our wedding, I had to remind myself that we didn't break Horror's number one rule. We weren't teenagers who lost control or secret lovers breaking vows. We were married. Sure, it was a little awkward at first, but it became…loving. Waking up in Sean's arms was a wonderful way to begin my next stage of life: graduated, married, and enrolled as a student of Heartford University. For the first time in my life, I truly felt successful, and I was excited for a grand future…with my loving husband.

Another month passed, then we received our reward from the HIU for defeating Dr. Hyde. Compiling our funds and Sean's inheritance from his parents, we were ready to tackle Sean's other impossible dream: emigration.

The paperwork to register for our passports almost felt like a Haunting. Just one problem after another. It didn't help that

I'd recently changed my last name, and Sean didn't have any of his birth records. Still, the frustration was lessened by the comfort from each other, and we persevered.

Meanwhile, we attempted to pack our whole lives into two checked bags, two carry-on suitcases, and personal bags. Sean wanted to take more, but I convinced him otherwise, explaining how "beloved trinkets" could turn into Hauntings. Besides, I hated our arguments spurred by "mine" and "yours" items that we'd both brought into the marriage. We sold them with plans to replace them when we settled into "our" new home.

It took the rest of the summer to organize our lives and transfers to Heartford University campus. Nearly five months after our Haunting in the woods, we were finally ready to go.

I left Gretta and Caroline with notes of gratitude and well wishes. *Always part ways with people and places on good terms,* Oz taught me. Would I miss Gretta's dry humor and Caroline's random trivia as much as I missed Oz's blank stares of quiet understanding? Probably not. Still, I cleared my throat of a growing lump as I took Sean's hand and headed for the International Airport of Inferno.

The security administrators made me empty my emergency pack, assuring me that their planes were "well equipped for emergencies and Hauntings." I grumbled, but followed their instructions to remove my revolver, stakes, and other "weapons" into a checked bag. They had us confirm again that we were in abatement, then pricked our fingers for blood to prove that we were alive and human before allowing us past security.

We joined a dozen wealthy emigrants on the small and turbulent propeller plane. Based on their formal clothes and various physical features, I guessed none of the other passengers were local Horrors. A collective sigh released as the wheels left the ground.

Once we landed in Romance, my eyes weren't wide enough to take in the scenes. People lined the terminal exit with signs, flowers, or balloons to greet specific people. Romantic women were somehow extra curvy, with hair that tumbled past their shoulders like soft curls of light, while the men's average body mass jumped. Many of them resembled Sean's fit physique, but I doubted they had his experience with fighting. Also, their skin tones were redder, blanched pink or sun-baked like ready-to-eat meat.

Sean squeezed my hand and chuckled at my wide stare. "You're not in Horror anymore, Pansy. We made it. Welcome to Romance."

At least...I wished that was how it happened.

Five Months After
the Camp-out

Despite my jetlag, I couldn't sleep during my first night in my new apartment in Heartford, Romance. Careful not to wake anyone, I snuck from my shared bedroom and into the kitchen with its adjoining living room. Everything from the non-faded floral curtains to the bright white lighting in this new apartment was foreign to me. The night was in full bloom, but no piercing screams, howling wind, or thunder broke the stillness. I checked outside, but it wasn't foggy either. In fact, the stars shone brightly, despite the city lights. Was that normal in Romance? The strangeness of it all was uncanny.

The quiet night only emphasized my loneliness.

Recalling advice from my grief counselor and hoping to ease myself, I found a piece of paper and began to write at the dining table.

Sean,

I did it. Today I managed to leave Horror and arrived in Heartford, Romance. Tomorrow, I'm starting classes in person I'm fulfilling your dream. It's all thanks to you. I only wish you were here with me.

I sniffed back my emotions to keep them from leaking, then continued.

If you were with me, then we'd live together in our own little apartment, and I'd feel safe. Because, even if my surroundings are foreign and unfamiliar, at least I'd have the familiarity of you beside me.

Wow, that sounded cheesy. Was this continent already affecting me? I considered erasing it, but decided it didn't matter. I planned to burn this letter, anyway.

Instead, I have new roommates, Heather Appleton (from Regency Romance) and Emma Morales (from Contemporary Romance). They're both the types of people who wouldn't have survived junior high in Horror. Seriously, Heather's clothes have way too many frills and layers, and were made for anything but running. And Emma...let's just say she reminds me of a fashion-minded Blake.

I'm writing this letter in the kitchen because both of them voted against my nightlight, saying it was "too bright." But how else do they expect to catch Hauntings sneaking up from the shadows? Did you really grow up around people like them?

I tapped my pencil thoughtfully as I tried to imagine Sean hanging around people like my new roommates or walking across Heartford University campus, as I had done earlier that evening. "I might have made one friend," I wrote.

Her name is Brooke Steamings. She's a year older than I am and rooming across the hall from me. She's from Steampunk, Sci-Fi, and speaks with an interesting accent. When she saw how "well" I was getting along with Heather and Emma, she invited me to join her at International Club. Sean, I wish you could have been there to see it. There were so many different types of people from all over the world! Brooke's friends included some girls from Children's and Mystery (at least, I think she was from Mystery because nothing about her made sense), and two guys from Western and Fantasy. They were all...very friendly. Like, unnervingly so. The Fantasy guy I don't remember his full name, but he called himself Theodor the Trusted... of all things! He was especially unnerving as he stared at me too much. I really hope he doesn't become my next Haunting. Based on his fancy title, mannerisms, and clothes, he seemed like someone with the authority to mess up my life.

Reflecting on Theodor and his awkward introductions, I squirmed. There was something…almost familiar about him that I couldn't name or place. The unknown notion tugged and prodded at me uncomfortably.

I needed to change subjects.

I wish you were here. You'd know what to do in this strange place you once called home. It's been five months. I thought I was healed from the way things ended, but this place reminds me so much of you.

But what's done is done. I can't change the past, but…I'll do everything I can to make the future better. Even if I need to do it myself, I will fulfill your dreams. I will become a paramedic and help as many people as I can. Just you watch…from wherever you are.

My lip quivered, and a sob nearly broke from me. Such a sound might wake my roommates. I managed to hold it back and let it leak from my eyes instead.

You once asked if I would cry over you. Well, I have. But they aren't happy tears like you wanted.

I'm sorry Sean

I loved you in the best way that I knew how. I'm sorry it wasn't enough. I really did want to marry you. I would have been perfectly happy and loyal to you forever. Wherever you are now, I hope you're at peace. And maybe, if there's any mercy in this world, maybe you'll find someone who can love you as much as you deserve.

I considered how to end the letter that I'd never send. I was over thinking it. Choosing simple honesty, I decided to end with a final note of gratitude.

Thanks for being more than a friend to me. You opened my eyes to the future and the world.
Love,
Pansy Finster

Writing Sean's Prequel

I'll admit, that first story is a bit dark, but it was set in Horror after all. Again, that was a prequel to *Don't Date the Haunted*, so if you want to see more from Pansy and her next haunted romance, look up the novel.

Those who've read *Don't Marry the Cursed* (book 2) may have recognized pieces of Chapter 1 of this novella. Writing the flashback in book 2 helped me to recognize the starting point for this story between Oz's death and meeting Sean at the orphanage.

The false ending of Chapter 24 was partially inspired by my readers wanting to know what happened next and by a specific conversation with another author who read *Don't Date the Haunted* then asked me, "If Pansy had married Sean before meeting Theo, would she have stayed loyal to Sean?" I'd never thought of it before, but I knew the answer was "Yes," if anything, because disloyalty is a major cause for Hauntings among adults. Chapter 24 was an exploration of that "What if…" It was also written as a replacement to an alternate ending of a scene after the events of *Don't Date the Haunted*. In my attempts to keep it vague, it still contained spoilers, so I removed it.

For more Behind the Scenes, the last few pages of Chapter 23 were originally written as a prologue to *Don't Date the Haunted*. That prologue received the most compliments from my writing group, and my first editor said, "Your first line is perfect. Simply perfect." Unfortunately, the same editor also told me that most people didn't read prologues, so I needed to either make it important or cut it.

I tried to make it important. I really did. I filled that little prologue with information about the poltergeist and mad scientist and cut later explanations in the book…but it felt forced. I even considered rewriting it as Chapter 1, but it didn't make sense to read about Pansy fighting the mad scientist Haunting, then Chapter 2 skipped five months to her new problems as she prepared to leave Horror.

So, goodbye prologue. In the writing community, we call this "Killing our Darlings." However, I'm terrible at killing my darlings and don't actually delete stories/scenes/or even sentences. I simply set them aside. Ever since cutting the prologue, I made early plans to expand the story into its own novella. Meaning, this little story has been years in the making as I explored Pansy and Sean's relationship through the Hauntings they faced.

I wrote a whole post about the deleted prologue on my website if you'd like to see an early draft and more details about the main inspiration for Sean's story.

https://craedarc.com/2020/11/13/behind-the-scenes-of-dont-date-the-haunted/

Simply put, there's a lot more where this came from.

Careful what you *Wish* for

A Prequel Short Story

Introduction

This next story is also a prequel to *Don't Date the Haunted*, but includes some minor spoilers by showing an alternate perspective of that book's Chapter 4.

If you hate horror stories and you skipped Sean's novella to this one, that's fine. They're completely separate stories. However, those who just finished that first story might recognize an event mentioned in that story's final chapter.

The scenes that made this story were originally written as an exercise to explore a main character's background while I was drafting *Don't Marry the Cursed*. Since book 2 is primarily about this character, his family, and his homeland, I needed to dive deeper into his reasons for leaving his homeland. Then, why did he choose Heartford, Romance, of all places, and what were his culture-shocks? Writing these scenes helped me to understand his motivations, background, and changing perspectives.

Unfortunately, combining the various scenes didn't make an actual story with an obvious conflict and resolution, so I trimmed it down to give it focus. I hope you enjoy *Careful What You Wish For*, a short story prequel from the perspective of Theodor, the Trusted, Lord of Margen, Fairytale, Fantasy.

Careful What You Wish For

I knew nothing about Ms. Pansy Finster when she first walked into my life, though I knew that she would make a fool out of me. I had waited for this moment from the time that I applied for Heartford University, never expecting it to actually happen.

I remembered my first day in Contemporary, Romance, stepping into my private suite, lugging my two large suitcases behind me and a large satchel around my shoulder. I missed the size and weightlessness of bottomless bags. Unfortunately, the magical item of Fantasy became a mere coin purse when crossing onto Romance soil. Thus, I was left to carry my luggage without even a levitating spell cast by a servant.

This was my lot for choosing to attend university in Romance instead of my homeland of Fairy, Fantasy.

I needed to step away from the looming reputation of my family. Not that their reputation was soiled in any way. Rather, the opposite as my father, brothers, and extended family were known for wielding incredible and powerful magical abilities… Then there was me, Theodor, the Trusted, second son of Duke Konrad Fromm, the only one in the entire royal family of Fairy to have a completely useless ability.

While my brothers had abilities to control wind, create darkness, and breathe fire, my ability to see meaningless auras left me struggling for influence. The people said they "trusted" me, yet no one listened to my opinions. I utterly failed in my attempts to win their respect with fighting skills. That left me with two more options: gain an influential education and marry an influential woman.

That led me to Heartford University in Contemporary, Romance. It had reputable professors and classes concerning international politics, and what better place to find True Love than Romance?

Founded in Contemporary, the university and campus accepted entry to both men and women. With its proximity to Regency, however, I suspected a fair amount of the attending women to be ladies of the court...and hopefully courtable ladies.

All I needed was Cupid to shoot me with one of his "two love-birds with one arrow."

I attempted to give Cupid a helping hand by courting women from my classes and nearby apartments, though I found them all ill-matched. I even tried a couple of "dates" with Contemporary women, knowing that my father would never approve of a commoner union.

I quickly realized that my ideal woman was a paradoxical dream. I wanted a refined woman with a title who would be satisfied with a "second best" lord, an independent woman who would depend on me (useless as I was) with Regency morals yet Contemporary enlightenment. I wanted someone who could believe in me even when no one else did.

I was a fool of a dreamer searching for a fantasy in Romance. Did such a woman even exist? How would I possibly find her without the help of Love at First Sight?

After receiving my Associate's degree and continuing for my Bachelor's in Political Science, I began attending the university's International Club. My initial hopes were to network with foreigners to strengthen my studies in international politics. My aims shifted as I found true friendships with Hank Hawkins from Western, Truth Locke from Mystery, Sally Johnson from Children's, and Brooke Steamings from Sci-Fi.

We were an oddball group with few commonalities other than our culture-shocks with Romance. While Hank appreciated the indoor plumbing and air conditioning, he thought the Romance landscape was boring. Truth commented on the bluntness of Romantic menus versus the round-about clues that Mysteries used. Brooke missed the ambient sounds of groaning gears and steampipe whistles, though she complimented the clean air of Heartford. I missed the variety of peoples (it was truly a travesty that fairies and half-breeds became plain humans outside of Fantasy), though I appreciated the equality of stations in Contemporary society.

In the summer between my Bachelor's and Master's degrees, I joined my friends for a camp-out in the woods of Regency. The historical grounds failed to support anything running on electricity, though (similar to my homeland) we found other forms of entertainment. We swam and played in the lake, made meals and treats over a campfire, then shared stories under the stars until shuffling into our separated tents.

On the last night of our trip, I wandered to the lakeshore, not wanting the adventure to end.

A snapping twig alerted me to Truth's approach behind me.

"Shoot," she swore. "I've gotten pretty good at sneaking and sleuthing in the city, but the woods have too much on the ground."

"Such as dirt and rocks and other definitions of 'ground?'" I laughed. She nudged me, then turned her attention to the brilliant sea of stars above us.

"Beautiful, aren't they?"

I grunted to vocalize my nod.

A bright light zipped across the sky, and Truth gasped. "Did you see that?"

"A shooting star."

Truth beamed like a child at Christmas. "Aren't you going to make a wish?"

I hid my unease the best I could. Wishes were not to be taken lightly. When Fantastics made wishes, they almost always came true, though rarely in the way the wisher intended.

I shrugged. "Brooke would probably say that such notions are foolish. Shooting stars are no more than comets passing. They cannot possibly know all the eyes that glimpse them. Also, what powers do they have for granting wishes?"

Truth pouted. "But she's a Sci-Fian. You're a Fantastic."

"And we are in Romance," I added.

She shrugged. "Why does that mean you can't make a wish? Isn't belief more important than nationality? I'd wager that a Sci-Fian who believes in wishes has more granted than a Fantastic who doesn't."

"Of course," I agreed, "because a Fantastic who disbelieves in wishes would never make a wish. Thus, by your statement, if a Sci-Fian makes a hundred wishes and has just one granted, they still receive more than the Fantastic who never wishes."

She snorted, an unfeminine trait that I found I appreciated. "Okay, fine, forget the statistics, but you still proved my point. How can you ever have a wish granted if you never try? So, stop talking, and let me concentrate on my wish."

I laughed and shook my head as she closed her eyes. In the silence of her wishing, I considered my own wish.

I did believe in wishes. To disbelieve in them would be unpatriotic to my homeland. Yet very few people knew their terrible truths. They were equal parts blessing and curse. A girl might wish to go to the ball, though only after she had been

142

worn out with chores and tears. A woman might wish for some money, though she might lose a precious heirloom as the cost. A father might wish for a newborn child, though he might lose his wife in the child's birth. One of the most commonly ignored warnings in Fantasy was to wish carefully.

That night, I made a wish.

I came to Romance for my education in hopes of finding a reputable wife. Thus far, I had only succeeded in my education while frustrating myself with the paradox of my ideal woman.

With that in mind, I made my wish as an utter fool. I wished to experience True Love at First Sight.

I considered possible ways for that wish to turn ugly on me. Perhaps she would be cursed? Curses could be broken. Perhaps she would be ugly? No, what would beauty matter as long as I loved her? Perhaps she was ill-fit for me? Then it would not be "true" love, would it?

Feeling secure with my wish, I threw it to the stars.

Then waited.

Nothing happened during that camping trip or when I visited home. The summer passed, and I forgot about the wish…until it hit me in the face.

I attended the first International Club meeting of my first graduate school year with Hank, meeting Truth and spotting Brooke as she entered. Brooke had brought a friend.

In a word, her friend was captivating. She was opposite in every way to my previous female acquaintances. I knew women with thick waves of gold rolling down their backs or tight curls of mousy browns. They had skin as white as snow and naïve faces, with round eyes and wide mouths.

The woman beside Brooke had black hair as a raven and cropped almost to a masculine length. She wore Contemporary faded jeans and a grey tank-top that showed off her toned figure in a rich shade of bronze. Her face was one of a hunter.

She was no wide-eyed doe of innocence. This woman knew a hard life, and she fought to be where and how she was.

The back of my mind scolded me for staring. The majority of my mind ignored the rebuke and continued to analyze her.

The most striking part about her was her aura. Almost everyone I met had relatively static blue-green auras, ranging between three and six centimeters while bouncing between lighter tints of two to four. This woman…she was something else. Her aura weaved in and out, shrinking down to a couple of centimeters, then blasting outward ten centimeters. The darkness of her aura remained around shades six or seven.

What was she doing to cause her aura to shift that way? Was she a witch? Merlin's beard, she was beautiful enough. I was willing to wager that she was a powerful one, too. Even if she was a murder hobo of Sword and Sorcery, perhaps my father would approve of a well-trained witch fighter.

If her aura was different from everyone else, perhaps that meant that *she* was different from everyone else. If I could discover what made her and her aura different, then I could discover the meaning behind my auras. Such a discovery could change my life. I would no longer be the useless son with a useless ability.

Within five seconds of analyzing her, my heartbeat quickened, my breath shortened, and I knew my life would never be the same. Except I wanted more than this strange woman to simply change my life. I wanted her to be a part of it forever.

As soon as that fact hit me, the compression on my chest increased ten-fold.

Curses, I was in love with a stranger. My wish had come true.

Brooke brought the dark-haired beauty towards our little group. During their approach, I bounced between ecstasy and terror. She came our way! Curses, what would I say? I could introduce myself and all my limited splendor then…what?

"Where have you been all my life?" "I know we just met, however, I think I love you." "What is your name? Fantastic! Will you marry me?"

Thankfully, Brooke provided our group with an introduction. "This is my new roommate, Pansy Finster, from Horror."

Pansy. My true love's name was Pansy Finster. From... Horror? The bloody ax decal on her "Hello, My Name is __Pansy__" sticker was verification. Merlin's beard. Of all the lands in Novel, I knew the least about Horror. Histories and rumors marked them as violent and tormented people; physically, verbally, mentally, and emotionally.

I watched as she exchanged polite greetings with Hank. Perhaps my prejudices were wrong. I swallowed hard and screwed my courage. Taking her nimble hand, I introduced myself and presented my most gracious bow; the one I usually reserved for my aunt, the Queen of Fairy. Only when I finished my introduction did I realize that I still had no idea what to say to her.

Curses—curses! What did people say to each other after experiencing Love at First Sight?

Right, Love at First Sight was a shared experience! Did she feel the same way that I did? Only one way to find out.

I asked, "Do you believe in Love at First Sight?"

She blinked her narrow brown eyes and slowly slipped her hand from mine. "Nnno."

No? *No?* What kind of cursed wish was this? How could love be true if I felt it alone? There had to be some mistake!

"Oh," I said. "What if we introduce ourselves again?"

Hank broke my focus with a loud laugh. The sound shook me back to reality and the insanity of my situation. I knew that I was a fool. I was a fool in love with a Horror who did not even believe in love. The God of Wishes had found a way to trick me, after all.

Very well. We citizens of Fairy were particularly known for turning bad situations to our favor. I just needed to use the old-fashioned way to make my own wish come true.

Heather's Haunted Summer Romance

#1.5 Novelette

Introduction

I prefer happy endings, so here's *Heather's Haunted Summer Romance.* Set in Romance and from Heather Appleton's perspective, it's the most romance-focused of these short stories, but still includes some seriously dark elements. Trigger warning: skip Chapter 6 if you're triggered by non-consensual kissing.

Don't know who Heather is? Don't worry, this novelette can stand alone. If you skipped the first two stories to come straight to this one, that's fine. Even though the events of this story happen between *Don't Date the Haunted* (book 1) and *Don't Marry the Cursed* (book 2), reading the first book isn't 100% necessary.

Although, beware: minor spoilers ahead (like certain characters who survived book 1, partial meaning behind a character's magical ability, and details on two relationships that are explored). That's all.

The main concept of this story came from the rules of Novel and the time gap between the first two books. In the world of Novel, citizens must face a form of conflict according to their land. As explained in Sean and Pansy's prequel, the people of Horror experience Hauntings, people of Romance experience Romances, and people of Fantasy experience Adventures. They aren't always the "main character" or Hero (as Fantastics put it), but situations occur every six to twelve months. Considering the eighteen-month gap between books 1&2, I realized Pansy's need to be involved in another Romance (as a minor role). Thus, *Heather's Haunted Summer Romance* was born.

Since *Don't Marry the Cursed* (book 2) took me four and a half years to write and publish, I had this novelette finished and available to quote. In Chapter 5 of book 2, you can find the reference, "last summer, when I helped Pansy save her room-mate…" (It continues with spoilers.)

Oddly enough, the most unbelievable parts of this story (Jake's off-screen actions) were inspired by real-life events. They were actually more ridiculous in reality, but I altered it to give Heather a different (and more believable) ending. I share this story with the permission of one of my best friends and roommates from university.

Enjoy.

Chapter 1

My mother was a traditional woman who believed that all Romances were beautiful. Growing up in Regency, Romance, I was inclined to agree. However, after a certain experience during my first summer as a student at Heartford University in Contemporary, Romance, my perspective became less naïve.

My bedroom door burst open, sending a tornado of air at me as I jumped with surprise in my vanity seat. I was not surprised, however, to see that it was only Pansy, my Horror-native roommate, sweating and red faced from her morning jog. She remained in the hallway and glanced around the room before entering. Approaching our first anniversary as roommates, I was nearly acquainted with her paranoid quirks. On a previous occasion, I had asked her to forewarn me of her barraging entrance.

She had stared at me with skepticism and said in her hushed accent, "But that would completely defeat the point."

The point of what? Giving me heart failure?

She stalked across our little room and peered between the window blinds from a suspicious angle. Being on the second floor gave us a little view of the street, lined with green grass and summer trees, surrounded by mountainous apartment buildings, local cafes, and small businesses that catered to weddings.

"Why's the window open?" my roommate asked. "Did you get dressed with the blinds slit like this? Have you seen anyone in the street?"

Questions, questions, questions. I could almost hear my mother's prim remark. *My dear, questions are to be asked sparingly and with care, like the slow drip of a well. Too many inquiries, one after another, will surely dry up the source of information, leaving you with only a few scant answers to quench your thirst for knowledge.*

My mother's voice of proper etiquette interrupted my thoughts less frequently as I immersed myself in the Contemporary side of Romance. All the same, she was there.

"It is July," I said. "The breeze is welcome, and the natural light is better when arranging one's hair."

"Then could you do your hair after you're fully dressed? People can see you."

I tilted my head to regard her own attire. She wore jogging shorts and a tank-top, her chin-length black hair pulled back with a headband, and her ever-present emergency pack strapped around her leg and hips.

"You jog around the neighborhood every other morning in that skimpy outfit, and you judge my modesty within our own bedroom? In the least, my sleeping gown covers my shoulders and knees."

"But you're from Regency. It's different when you show it."

I raised an eyebrow to her.

She sighed. "Look, I don't feel comfortable in this room. I feel like we're being watched."

"Ah, is that why you made a habit of dressing in the bathroom?" I pondered aloud. "What a relief. I thought that perhaps you missed the stench as your bed no longer borders the toilets."

"Ew, no." She scrunched her nose. "The junior room is much nicer than the freshman room. But as Stacy and I rounded the block coming home, I thought I saw someone looking up at our window."

I leaned on my seat to peer outside, suddenly curious. However, something else in Pansy's words caught my attention.

"You went running with Stacy?" Stacy was a new roommate and one of the few who stayed for the summer. As one raised in Children's, she was inundated with cheery energy.

Pansy shifted her weight in an uncomfortable manner. "Yeah, she's been running on her own, but people should run with partners. Since Theo's in classes, I went with her."

Her bitter tone and darting glances suggested more was on her mind. "I sense that your uneasiness concerns more than our open window."

She opened her mouth to argue, but stuttered and relented. "No, you're right. I hoped to get it out during my run, but I can't talk with Stacy about it."

I patted her bed nearby to encourage her to sit and talk with me. As she came nearer, I regretted the action and fought back a grimace. Pansy must have run harder than usual. She had a rather distasteful odor about her. I pumped my perfume then busied myself with my hair-do to distract my expressions.

"I don't know what to do about Theo," she said, collapsing onto her bed. "Ever since he came back from his trip to Fantasy, our relationship has been…complicated."

I frowned. "That was two months ago."

"Yeah, I know, but…I'm busy with school to graduate next spring, and he spends his weekends researching for his Master's Thesis. It gives us no time together. And…and I don't know if we could ever work it out. I accidentally brought up marriage yesterday, and it hit me why we never could. I hate the idea of breaking up, but we'll have to face reality, eventually."

I froze with my hands in the middle of a pinning. Pansy and Theo break up? It was unfathomable! They loved one another! They were a perfect match! Any Romantic could see…except Pansy was no Romantic.

"Why would you be forced to break up?"

"Because he's a royal Fantastic, and I'm only a Horror," she said bitterly.

I waited for more, but she offered no explanation even as I finished with my hair. Stowing my pins away, I grabbed my breakfast apple and urged, "I fail to see how that makes you Romeo and Juliet."

"Well," she flustered, "next year we're graduating, and he'll return to Fantasy…permanently. He wants to help his family rule a duchy and be surrounded by other people with magical abilities. I don't even know what my plans are yet, but I don't plan to return to Horror, and I can't be with Theo in Fantasy."

"Why ever not?" I asked between apple bites.

Pansy wiped her sweaty palms down her shorts and long legs. "Theo's aunt is the Queen of Fairy, Fantasy. He's royalty, meaning anyone he marries will become a Lady of Fairy. Can you imagine me as a lady?" She barked a bitter laugh. Indeed, I had a hard time imagining her in a delicate gown, gracing a curtsy to a frog prince.

As if to prove my point, she unceremoniously dumped her emergency pack across her bed. Counting her collection of matches, stakes, and silver bullets, she said, "I've never been responsible for anyone more than myself, not to mention a million people I've never met in a land I've never seen. And what would I do there? I don't have magic. I can work as a paramedic pretty much anywhere *except* Fantasy. My goal was to work with a Contemporary Romance, Thriller, or a Mystery hospital. I could even go to Sci-Fi, but that would require extra schooling for their equipment and alien biology. I'd probably need to add a minor in pediatrics before trying for Children's, but I'd prefer that over the limited supplies and support of Western or any Regency states…no offense."

"None taken," I said with a wave of my hand. I knew the limits of my homeland. That was why I came to Contemporary for my education. Though, for Pansy, the whole world was open to her like a book—no, like a library.

She sighed, finishing her daily verification of weapons and began repacking her emergency bag. "The one place I imagine my medical training being useless is Fantasy. They don't need medics. They're stuck in the dark ages of medicine because they have magical abilities, spells, potions, and witchcraft to fix their ulcers." With each word, her voice became more bitter until she grimaced with contempt.

I gave her a tested smile. "You may not be as 'useless' as you think. Remember when Theo thought his magical ability was useless? Yet we discovered that his sight of auras was incredibly useful after you learned of its capacity to show when a person was in danger."

She grunted, an unsophisticated sound to express her attitude.

"Have you discussed your concerns with Theo?" I asked.

She leaned back with a groan of frustration. "Not really. I'm worried that if I do, he'll drop everything he's ever worked for to make me happy. But does that mean I need to drop everything I've worked for to make him happy? Ugh! Love is so dumb sometimes!"

I agreed wholeheartedly with her exclamation. "Regardless," I said, "you and Theo are perfect for each other. You mutually share love and trust for one another."

"What about you and Jake? I thought you two were perfect for each other, but…"

She left her argument unfinished, allowing my thoughts to drift into pleasant memories and possibilities of what could have been. I had thought Jake was perfect for me, too. Born in Regency, but raised in Contemporary, Jacob Kennington understood and graced me with "old fashioned" respect, though also treated me with the equality that came with Contemporary ideas. We had courted through the entirety of the school year, despite my parents' disapproval of his lower-class family and desired occupation as a journalist.

I had no problem defying them for the sake of love, though his desires to travel the world and delay a family sat uneasily with me. Then he announced his internship in New Angeles, Erotica, for the summer. With mutual agreement, we broke off our courtship.

Yet we remained friends as he regularly phoned me, inadvertently reminding me how I secretly still loved him. I hoped that feeling was also mutual as he promised not to date anyone during his internship, though he encouraged me to consider other men. Not that I had any offers.

"Has he called you yet this week?" Pansy asked.

I sighed and tossed my apple core to the trash bin. "We spoke last night."

"Then he told you about his first kiss?"

"His what?" I stumbled in my motion to stand.

Take care to be more graceful, my mother chided.

"Oh," Pansy shuffled awkwardly. "Wait, then he didn't tell you? I'm sorry, I thought you knew. I actually heard about it from Hank that Jake posted it on his social media. Oh, right. You don't use social media. But I thought he'd tell you since you call regularly."

"He posted about it on social media?" Yet he neglected to tell me even as we spoke last night?

"According to Hank, Jake changed his status to 'in a relationship' with a fellow intern who tagged him in a story about some Erotica tradition for people to kiss by a monument under the full moon. The werewolf moon was three days ago.”

It was too much. I grabbed my school pack and turned around to hide my face. No styling of hair could disguise the emotions I felt.

“I’m sorry, Heather, I thought you knew!” Pansy called to me as I walked out the door and up to campus.

Chapter 2

A woman must control her emotions, my mother reprimanded. *She is not allowed to feel offended by anyone. She must accept offenses as charges to become better.*

Except the gall of that man! How *dare* he? My class began in ten minutes, but I knew any concentration for my studies was lost. I decided to rush up to class, then call him from a campus phone for the truth.

Fuming as I was, I rounded the corner of a building and bumped right into someone. A bouquet of flowers burst before me and fluttered to the ground.

"Pardon me," I flustered. "Allow me to help."

I crouched to the ground to help the gentleman pick up his flowers. The breed of flowers caused me to pause in surprise.

"These are heather flowers," I said.

"Yes." The man looked up and his eyes met mine. Dark blue like an untamed sea, sandy blonde hair like the perfect beach, pristine posture like someone of noble blood, all wrapped up in a handsome grey vest with no overcoat. Never before had I seen a man of such perfect creation.

True love at first sight, my mother would have called it. *When you least expect it, you meet someone and instantly know.*

"I-I'm sorry," he bent his face away to collect his dismantled bouquet.

"Oh, I should be the one to apologize," I said. "I was distracted and I ruined your beautiful bouquet."

He smiled lightly and spoke in a rush. "They're for my grandmother. She's sick, but these half-trampled flowers might wilt her spirit further."

"Oh no! Is there anything I can do to pardon myself?" I collected the last stem and handed it to him. He smiled as our hands touched. A shiver ran through me unlike any I had felt before.

"As long as you're offering..." He shuffled his feet. "I can't give her this bushel. How about you take them off my hands?"

"Surely there are plenty of stems in here that may appease your grandmother. I need not take them all."

"I insist," he said, offering the bouquet to me. His eyes didn't leave me another option. They were intensely focused on me. Never before had a man stared at me in such a way before. I was flattered, yet unsure what he meant by it.

"What's your name?"

"Miss Heather Appleton."

"Heather," he repeated, surprising me that he assumed the intimacy of my first name. He glanced at the heather flowers in his hand, then smiled. "Do you believe in fate?"

"I believe the timing and circumstances of this meeting have been no small coincidence."

His smile widened. "I agree. Can I take you to dinner tomorrow?"

My breath caught in my throat. "Such forwardness, good sir. I do not even know your name."

"Lew. Lew Hunsaker. And dinner?"

The thought of a date clenched my heart with worry. I only just met this man. And Jake — Jake could go and have a good life on his own for all I cared. How dare he kiss another woman and not have the nerve to tell me? Then to blurt it to the world on his social media? The gall!

"I would be delighted, Mr. Hunsaker. I reside in the Psi Dormitories if you would like to pick me up at seven o'clock."

"I'll see you then."

Mr. Hunsaker graced me with another dazzling smile before I headed off to classes. I had no time to call Jake before class. I decided to call him after and hope he had a decent excuse for his behavior.

Chapter 3

"He said *what?*" Pansy's face dropped in disbelief. The amount of ice cream that filled my mouth made answering difficult. My mother would have been appalled, saying, *Eat with decorum and chew discreetly, my dear.*

Seeing my occupation, my roommate continued, "Let me get this straight; you and Jake dated for eight months without kissing, then he promised not to date anyone during his internship. Then he kisses someone. on. his. internship! Does he want some epic with that *fail?*"

"If only that was his worst offense," I muttered. "When I asked if he loved her, he refused to answer, instead providing the most pathetic of distractions, saying, 'Oh, look a tree.'"

Pansy threw her hands in the air as if giving up on humanity. "Are you serious? Who says that? Please tell me you gave him a piece of your mind!"

"I did." I took another spoonful of ice cream to obscure my embarrassed smile. His refusal to answer either meant that he did love her and was too embarrassed to tell me, even as a friend, or that he did not love her and had kissed her without honesty. "I called him the worst possible name I could imagine."

"Oh, this better be good." Pansy buckled down with eagerness. "What did you say?"

"I called him a man-whore."

My best friend burst into laughter.

Boisterous laughter is hardly lady-like. To be a gentlewoman means to be gentle in all expressions.

I pushed aside my mother's rules to enjoy the moment of bitter indulgence. I was indeed grateful that Pansy had different opinions as I recounted what occurred. Instead of breaking with joviality, my mother would have scolded me for my crude and slanderous language.

"So, if I'm picturing this right," my roommate said between heavy breaths, "you're on the public phone, right outside the doors to the library, and you shout the words, 'You man-whore!'"

She broke into another round of laughter. This time, I joined her with embarrassed giggles.

I was both ashamed and proud of my brazen exclamation. "I did catch a few stares."

"Oh, that's brilliant. Can we remember this day forever? The day Jake epically failed, and you gave it to him."

Pansy took a delightful bite of ice cream and closed her eyes as if to seal the memory.

"I know not what to tell him," I whispered. Pansy opened her eyes to stare at me.

"Tell him he's an idiot and deserves a chainsaw accident in a particular area."

I grimaced. "Do I encourage him to date her, then?"

Pansy's face opened with surprise. Then, thinking it over, she sighed and leaned back. "If you do, you're a good person and deserve better than someone like him. What about this other guy, Lew? You just 'happened' to run into him, and he just 'happened' to have a bouquet of heather flowers to hand you? Things like that don't just 'happen' in real life. Your life is unreal."

"It is not uncommon in Romance for the stars to align just perfectly."

Pansy sighed and shook her head. "I can't trust it. It's *too* perfect. Don't you ever worry?"

"For what cause?" I asked. "Men in Romance do not turn into poltergeists or mass murderers, Pansy. This is not Horror."

"I know, but..." She paused as she struggled internally. "Nevermind, you're right. I need to follow my brother's last counsel and stop being so paranoid. You have a date tomorrow?"

"Yes, he is taking me for dinner. Would you help me to prepare?"

Pansy lifted an unsure smile. "You know I'm the last person who should give dating advice."

"Yet which of us has been previously engaged and is now in a steady courtship?"

She frowned. "And going nowhere. I really need to talk to Theo."

Instant panic rose within me. "You plan to break your courtship with Lord Fromm?"

She moaned, "I don't know. That's why we need to talk. I love Theo, and even the thought of breaking up with him tears me apart, but...I can't just drop everything I've ever worked for, everything I *know*, and follow him to some far away castle."

I pursed my lips. "You haven't the faintest idea how many women would grovel for such an opportunity."

Pansy sighed. "I know. That's another reason I think we need to break up. He deserves better. He deserves someone noble like him, someone who knows magic—or has an ability like his. Condemnation, he deserves a princess!"

"Pansy—" I set aside my ice cream to take her hands "—he deserves love, and that is what you can give him. He deserves someone who believed in him even when he doubted himself. He deserves someone who has put his life before her own.

Then, regardless of all that, he *chose* you. Does he not deserve to choose?"

She busied her mouth with more ice cream rather than to reply. I took my own bite and waited, determined to hold firm. She swallowed and refused to meet my gaze.

"I don't know," she said. "We'll have some time to talk tomorrow after his classes. We still have a lot to figure out."

Chapter 4

Pansy and I spent the rest of the evening with a Romantic film, both of us wishing our lives were as simple as those portrayed on the screen. She helped me to prepare for my date the following day as we took a girl's day in town to pamper ourselves with manicures and facials. Pansy looked glamorous even in her faded jeans and utilitarian jacket. I envied her thick and straight hair, strong facial structure, dark and toned body build, and beautiful…everything. A part of me was glad she was a little strange and already spoken for. Otherwise, I imagined men clamoring for her attention.

During the pampering and lulls in conversation, my mind wandered to Jake. Tried as I did to banish that traitor from my thoughts, my first love crept through the corners of my mind. Thoughts of Jake guilted me about my date with Mr. Hunsaker. Even though he encouraged me to see other people, this was my first time to test his advice.

I mentally shook my head. Jake had a new love interest. He had moved on, and even kissed her. It was my turn to move ahead and focus on someone new.

I imagined Mr. Hunsaker with his shy smile and bouquet of heather flowers. My mind wandered into a daydream I'd frequently had of Jake. With effort, I replaced it with Mr. Hunsaker, sweeping me off of my feet during a holiday celebration in the rain, and my heart would be his with a gentle press of his lips.

Pansy asked me for an opinion on her nail color, bringing me back to reality with heated cheeks. *Mind your musings, my dear, for thoughts have a curious way of transforming into deeds. One should guard the mind as vigilantly as one guards the heart.*

I finished my preparations at home, selecting, unselecting, then reselecting my outfit four times before scrambling with limited time.

Mr. Lew Hunsaker arrived ten minutes early for our date. Pansy opened the door, expecting Theo. She kept Mr. Hunsaker standing on the porch until I came from our bedroom, my accessories still in need of last minute touches.

"I have only a couple more things to prepare," I said. "Pansy, there is no need to make him wait outside. Please, come in." I swung the door wide from Pansy's inch-wide gap. She narrowed her eyes at Lew as he stepped over the threshold.

"Please, forgive my roommate," I said to Mr. Hunsaker as an introduction. "This is Pansy. She came from Horror and has this tendency to leave people standing outside. I believe it has something to do with vampires."

Mr. Hunsaker laughed uncomfortably, rubbing his hands nervously against his dress slacks.

"I shall only be a few more minutes," I said, excusing myself back to my room.

He spoke loudly so I could hear, "As long as we don't lose our reservation."

"Reservation?" I pondered aloud. "Where are we going? I do hope to be dressed well enough."

"You look beautiful," he said, much closer than I expected.

I jumped with a small shriek to find Mr. Hunsaker standing at my bedroom doorway. He was half hidden by the frame as he stared at me with wide eyes.

166

"Was that a *real* shriek?" Pansy popped her head around the other side of the door frame to check on me.

"I am alright. Mr. Hunsaker," I scolded, "it would be more appropriate if you waited in the living room."

"I wanted to wa—talk to you as you got ready."

"Oh. Um…I suppose that may be fine." That was a new experience. My fingers fumbled under his watch. I gave up and moved to gathering my purse supplies. Compact versions of my perfume, extra hair pins, a hand fan, feminine products (just in case), wallet, and keys.

I eyed the unused pepper-spray that Pansy gifted me for my birthday. Such an odd present. I looked to Mr. Hunsaker and decided against it. His large arms were probably more than enough to protect me for the night.

Mr. Hunsaker offered his arm to escort me, and I waved goodbye to Pansy. Her wary eyes frowned, the way they always did when she met someone new.

I sighed at her worries. "I shall return before midnight. Correct, Mr. Hunsaker?"

"Of course," he scoffed at Pansy's mothering.

Her shoulders relaxed, and she offered a quick smile. "Don't have too much fun."

"Not without you," I said to answer the light tease.

Mr. Hunsaker said our destination was close, thus we walked side by side toward campus. I thought to ask where our reservations were, but allowed the surprise to taunt me. I made some guesses based on our walk and the direction we took. There were only so many restaurants near campus that took reservations.

"Are we dining at the Top Tier?" I gasped.

"We are." He grinned. "I've heard great reviews about the place."

"Have you never been?" I asked.

"Not yet."

I beamed with excitement. "Oh, you will love it! It is my favorite place to eat near campus! I would eat there every day if I could!"

"Would you?" he laughed. "Then I'm glad I chose it."

We were seated at a small table for two and asked what we would like to drink.

Mr. Hunsaker spoke first, "Two lemon teas, please, with some honey for the lady."

I blinked in surprise. "Thank you. I do enjoy lemon tea, especially with honey."

He ducked shyly. "Oh, good. I thought it compliments your sweetness."

I blushed and hid my face with my menu. I knew what I wanted, though I needed a distraction from ogling at the perfect man across from me.

When the waiter returned with our teas, Mr. Hunsaker said we were ready to order. I looked up, surprised again. I had said nothing about making a choice.

"I would like the clam chowder with the potatoes and bread bowl," he said.

I grinned. "Good choice. Their clam chowder bread bowl is particularly delicious. I get it almost every time I come here."

"Do you?" He smiled back, nervous and excited.

I addressed the waiter to switch my potatoes for steamed vegetables, then he collected our menus and left for the kitchens. Without the reading distraction, I sipped my tea and struggled to contain my patience. There were so many questions to ask, such as where had he been all my life?

A woman must let the man speak first. Better to let him direct the conversation that you may know it will interest him.

"Um…" He rubbed his hands again. "Heather…I've been… looking forward to meeting you."

I hesitated, wondering what he meant by that. Unable to determine, I asked, "In what way?"

"Well…" He grabbed his napkin and balled it in his hands. "I never thought I'd actually meet someone like you."

My breath caught at his sincerity. "You are too kind, Mr. Hunsaker. There are many women like me—"

He shook his head before I finished. "No. You are one of a kind, Heather. I've never known a woman as nice as you."

"You hardly know me at all." I smiled, my heart bleeding out for this dear man.

"I would like to change that." He grinned back with eager anticipation. "I want to know everything about you, Heather. And I want you to call me Lew."

I glanced down at the napkin on my lap to hide my blush. "If you desire it…Lew."

We nibbled on our salads until our clam chowder soup bowls arrived. Lew must have been familiar with the advice to encourage a woman to talk about herself, because he asked me many questions about my upbringing, my family, my classes, and likes and dislikes. He agreed with so many of them, I wondered if we were secretly the same person. Whenever I tried to ask a question about him, he answered briefly, then found a way to turn it back on me.

In so many ways, he reminded me of Jake with his Regency courtesies, yet the Contemporary humor. No, I needed to forget about Jake, as he had clearly forgotten about me. I focused on the perfect man before me and replayed my daydream of a holiday kiss in the rain, featuring Lew.

Chapter 5

Three and a half hours flew by as we stayed for dessert and lingered long enough to finish what would have been leftovers. I wondered if Lew had any other plans for our date, though as the night wore on, we ran out of time for a second activity.

It was an hour before midnight when Lew suggested walking me home. "Sorry for keeping you so long, but it's been really nice to talk to you. I feel like I could go on forever, just to hear your voice."

I blushed, feeling guilty that the conversation had been more of a question-and-answer interview.

He offered his jacket for me to wear in the chilled summer night, which I gratefully accepted. When his arm remained around my shoulders, however, I stepped away. I was not quite ready for such Contemporary casualness. That set us in an awkward mood, and little was said during the walk back.

Approaching the Psi Dormitory, I spotted Pansy one step beyond the porch threshold. She was saying a prolonged goodnight with a tall dark-haired man wearing a medieval tunic embroidered with Fairy emblems. Pansy and Theo held hands and spoke so quietly that I could not hear. Relief settled into my heart as they said goodnight with a quick kiss.

They were still together then. Good.

Pansy went deeper inside, and Theo came our way to head home. He walked with heavy feet. Even if their courtship continued, Theo was still troubled. It pained my heart to think of what Pansy said to make him so down-trodden. Then his eyes met mine, and he jerked back with surprise.

"Heather!"

Lew's arm wrapped around my shoulders again. Did he feel the need to protect me from Theo?

Hoping to ease his concerns, I introduced them. "Lew Hunsaker, this is my friend, Lord Theodor Fromm."

"Friend?" Lew questioned. "I saw the way you watched him with that other girl."

"Yes, *friend*," I reaffirmed, surprised by Lew's sudden and intense jealousy. "He is in a courtship with my roommate. I am merely concerned for their happiness together."

Undeterred, Lew drew himself up to Theo. "Who are you really? Are you dating the roommate only to get closer to Heather?"

Theo straightened and met Lew's shorter challenge. "I am Lord Theodor Fromm, the Trusted, of Margen. Heather already explained our friendship. What reason do you have to discredit her words?"

"Well, Mr. Lord, the beautiful Heather and I are on a date tonight, so you'll have to wait your turn."

Theo's eyes narrowed until he turned to me, and his eyes softened. "Are you alright, Heather?"

"She's fine," Lew snarled.

"I prefer to hear reassurance from her own lips," Theo said.

Lew raised his chin, as if to make himself taller than Theo's hundred and eighty-plus centimeters. "I'm sure an unworthy man like yourself wants more than just reassurance from Heather's angelic lips."

"Lew!" I gasped at his audacity.

Theo sneered at Lew with distaste, an expression I had never seen him wear before. "Miss Appleton is my friend. Even if she was not, she is my beloved's best friend, and I would respect her for Pansy's sake. I am merely concerned for Miss Appleton's *safety*." He shot a look at me—no—at my aura! Did he see that I was in danger? From what?

"I am well enough," I said, hoping to dissolve the tension. "We will finish here shortly."

Theo clenched his jaw, dissatisfied, but nodded and turned back towards the street. I watched him until Lew jerked my arm, probably harder than he intended, and led me to the Psi Dormitory front porch.

"Thank you, Lew, for tonight," I said, rummaging through my purse for my dorm key. "Dinner was lovely."

That was entirely true. The food and setting had been perfect. The date as a whole, however, began to unnerve me. I looked forward to a departure with a kiss on the hand, then to talk it out with Pansy. She probably knew how to handle this situation…whatever it was.

Lew watched me rummage through my purse. "Sorry for that interruption. I don't want to say goodbye already. Is that wrong?"

I looked up, surprised by his tenderness.

"It's just…" He paused to collect his words. "This evening has been like a dream come true. I'm not ready for it to end. You promised your roommate you'd be back by midnight, right? We still have a half hour. Can we walk around a bit?"

The slippers on my feet were made more for elegance than walking, but perhaps he wanted to end on a happier note than the incident with Theo. We still had a half hour before our predetermined curfew, so I allowed the extension. What harm could a walk do?

As we walked, Lew offered his arm to escort me, and I took it, remembering strolls with Jake through gardens. No, I needed to stop thinking of him and how he always matched my pace, how his mouth crinkled with laughter at the cheesiest of jokes, or how his eyes —

Stop!

"This is where I live," Lew said, thankfully distracting me. He gestured to a small three-storied apartment complex built of Heartford's historical red brick. We were only a block or so away from my dormitory.

"Actually," Lew said, shuffling sheepishly, "I have a gift for you inside. Would you like to see it?"

A gift? "I suppose," I said, curious.

With my hand still at his elbow, he rested his other hand over mine, almost as if he was scared that I would leave him. I saw no reason for it and let him guide me inside. He led me through a hallway and simple door until I found myself in a living room with a TV and a telescope by the window.

Lew stepped away to another room. "Give me a second. I'll be back."

I excused him with a nod, unsure about an uneasy feeling in my core. I removed Lew's jacket from my shoulders and thought to distract myself with the telescope. Even if the view was obstructed from the ground level in the city, looking at the stars always put me at ease.

Except, what I saw through the spyglass was not stars and not easing. I found myself spying into an apartment window at a young woman with short dark hair and a grey tank top, talking on a flip phone. Pansy. My roommate. Why was Lew's telescope focused on my bedroom window?

I recalled Pansy's paranoid warnings of someone watching through the window. Chills crawled up my skin, and I recognized the feeling—the creepiness. I had never felt such chills before meeting Lew, but felt them every time I was with him.

Was this how Pansy felt about everyone? No wonder she was paranoid!

I flinched back from the eyepiece, squeaking the telescope out of position. In the silence of the apartment, he probably heard that and would come to investigate the sound.

Panic struck my heart and doubled as the eerie quietness of Lew's apartment sank into my bones. Where were his roommates? Surveying my surroundings again, I found only one chair at the kitchen table.

I was alone in a man's home? My reputation was ruined! How long had I been there? Did anyone see me enter?

On one hand, I feared the shame that would blemish my name if someone knew of my intimate whereabouts. On the other, I hoped someone respectable would know to rescue me if necessary.

"Heather?" Lew!

He re-entered the room with a little box. He caught me in the middle of my escape to the front door. His eyes bounced between my terrified expression and the repositioned telescope. For a moment, he seemed as terrified as I felt. Then he swallowed and squared his shoulders.

"Please don't leave, Heather. Not now," he said, approaching me like I was some feral animal. "Not now that you know how much I love you."

Chapter 6

"Love me?" I gasped, my breath tight with fear. "You hardly know me. While I might have admired you, we are yet strangers!"

"But that's the thing, Heather—"

"Miss Appleton," I corrected, determined to return to the formal courtesies of Regency mannerisms.

He ignored me and continued to step closer. "I'm more than fond of you, and you're no stranger to me. I kiss the ground you walk on." How vomitous. "I knew your first name was Heather, like the flowers." Then he'd set up our first meeting? "I reserved dinner at the Top Tier because I knew it was your favorite restaurant." Meaning he'd watched me even after I'd left my apartment. "I knew your favorite meal and drink, and how you prefer your men to look and act." Did that mean he knew about Jake? "I did all of this for you."

I matched his forward movements with my own backward until I hit the wall. Only a little farther, and I could reach for the door. Admittedly, I had often daydreamed of having a secret admirer, but this…this was beyond admiration or any healthy standard of a relationship. "Why?" I found myself asking. "Why me?"

"As I said, I love you, Heather. I can hardly take my eyes off you." He leapt for the door as I reached for it. His fingers smashed my hand as he threw me aside and away from the door.

I landed on the hem of my gown and stumbled into a wooden nightstand on my way to the floor. My dress ripped at the waist seam, and I scraped my forearm in my landing.

After locking his front door, Mr. Hunsaker ran to my side. "Heather—"

"Miss Appleton," I snapped and edged away from him.

"Are you hurt? I'm sorry, I didn't mean to hurt you. I would never hurt you."

"Then let me go home."

His eyes turned pitiful, like a scorned puppy. "But you're hurt. Let me take care of you."

"No, I think not," I said. I was obviously well enough to walk, and I doubted he had better medical supplies or experience than Pansy with her paramedic training.

"Please," he whispered, leaning towards me. "Let me kiss it better."

Dear heavens — "If you do, I'll scream."

"I'd like to hear you scream." His eyes zeroed on my mouth with a wild hunger. I scrambled back, but my sprawling skirts kept me from shuffling far. He lunged for me, gripping the back of my neck and shoving his mouth against mine. For a moment, I was too shocked to do anything. This was my first kiss? The wrongness of it all made me want to cry.

I squealed through my nose, but Lew's moans of pleasure were louder. I opened my mouth to scream. That was a mistake. Lew's lips followed mine, then some giant wet thing rolled into and around my mouth.

What was that? Heavens above! Was that his *tongue?*

I screamed, and Lew laughed. He laughed! How did this happen? Everything was so wrong! What happened to the perfect gentleman from this evening? Had it all been a farce to trick me?

He crushed my mouth with his again—Oh, dear heavens, why was this happening? I tried to slap him away, but he pinned my arms to my sides. I cried, and Lew held me in an abusive embrace. Each minute could have been an hour for all the horror that raced through my mind.

Horror. Pansy probably knew what to do in a situation like this. What would Pansy do?

Fight back.

I bit down on Lew's tongue. He jerked back and finally retracted his mouth from mine.

"Ow!"

"Let me go! Stop!"

"But I love you, Heather!"

"You man-whore! If you love me, then let me go home!"

He had the nerve to chuckle. "Man-whore? But I would never be unfaithful to you."

"You are unfaithful now to my respectability! Let me go, you are hurting me!"

"I don't want to hurt you, Heather. I love you, and promise to make you happy. If only you stop struggling, you'll see."

"Let me go!" I cried.

He leaned down with his slobbery lips again, and I turned my head away, screaming as loud and high as I could. He went for my neck, right below my jaw, and sucked on my skin. Screaming became easier.

A loud knock threatened to burst down the front door.

Chapter 7

Muffled voices called, "Let her go!"

"Open this door, right now! The police are on their way!"

"Heather! What's going on?"

A glimmer of hope leaked into my sobbing. I recognized those voices. Friends. People who loved me, truly loved me, without lust or creepy fascination.

"Help me!" I cried.

Mr. Hunsaker growled and finally rolled away from me. This was my chance to escape. Mr. Hunsaker blocked the front exit as he began a shouting argument with masculine voices muffled behind doors and walls. Careful not to catch his attention, I crawled back. I wanted a door and wall between myself and the monster before me.

With only one step between me and the next room and three steps between me and Mr. Hunsaker, I scrambled to my feet and dashed into the room.

Mr. Hunsaker shouted, "Hey, wait!" as I slammed the door between us. Thankfully, there was a lock on my side. I doubted the tiny switch would hold him for long.

Surveying my new surroundings gave me little hope. I had managed to lock myself in his bedroom with pictures of cars and female models on the walls. There was a window, how-ever, and we were on the ground level. Could I escape through the window? Seeing no other option, I gritted my teeth and hefted up my multiple skirt layers.

A soft knock on the window almost sent me jumping out of my skin. I yanked up the blinds to find Pansy angled to the side.

"Pansy!"

She jabbed a finger to her lips to shush me. How could she expect me to be quiet at a time like this?

I unlocked the window and threw it open with a screech. Pansy cringed.

The door handle jiggled, and I pushed against the window screen.

"Push on the edges!" Pansy instructed. "Hurry!"

I shoved one corner free from the window frame when the door broke open. I turned just in time to see Mr. Hunsaker's face. He was both livid and terrified, although not nearly as terrified as I was. I had no sympathy.

"No!" he shouted and grabbed at me. "Don't leave me now! Tell them to go away! I won't hurt you!"

"Let go of me!" I tried to wiggle my arms free, but he had me in a vice-like grip.

Pansy shouted from outside, "Hold on, Heather!"

Hold on to what? He was the one holding on, and I wanted him to let go!

A crack of plastic against wood broke around the window as Pansy wrenched the screen away. Mr. Hunsaker backed away with me still in his arms as the Horror hefted herself through the window. The glare she gave him was, indeed, horrifying. Her lips were pinched into a non-existent line of fierce determination while her eyes flamed with warning and vengeance.

"You can't touch me while I have Heather!" he threatened.

With one swift swoop to rival the speed of a Westerner's quick draw, Pansy pulled her revolver from her emergency pack and aimed it directly at his face. He screamed like a young maid.

He shoved me at Pansy and scrambled through the bedroom door, still screaming.

"Heather!" a man shouted from beyond the front door. "Is that you? What's going on? Don't worry, the police are here!"

I held tightly onto Pansy as she kept her gun trained on the bedroom doorway in case Mr. Hunsaker came back. Seeing no escape, he ran around his apartment like a beheaded chicken. Lights flashed across the windows, and more voices joined the front door.

"Open up, this is the police!"

My attacker resorted to the fetal position on the floor, rocking back and forth on his bottom.

"Everything is ruined!" he muttered, eyes shifting between pleading to me and begging to Pansy. "It wasn't supposed to be like this, I just—I just wanted—I didn't want—this wasn't supposed to happen…"

I tried to gesture to the front door. My fingers trembled. Good grief, all of me trembled!

"Should we not let them in?" I asked.

"No," Pansy said, her voice remarkably calm. How was she calm? "We have a good position here. We have multiple exits, and I have a direct sight on your Haunting. If we move, we'll make ourselves vulnerable to traps or outside forces. Those outside can break down the door and cross the threshold on their own."

I understood little between the chaos, but would follow Pansy's survival experience. The front door barged down. I jumped, Pansy twitched, and Mr. Hunsaker yelped.

What followed was a bit of a blur. Lights flashed around the apartment, scoping every corner, blinding me multiple times as they searched our faces. Two men rushed our way, and arms wrapped around us.

"Pansy! Heather!" Theo breathed with relief. "Thank the gods, your auras have safer tints."

Another man wrapped me within his arms and held me tenderly. He spoke of sweet worries and grateful praises. Wait a minute. I knew that voice. I knew that cologne and that tender embrace…

I rocked back. "Jake!"

"Let's take you home."

"Please," I sighed, almost sobbing with relief.

The police wanted each of our accounts and perspectives of what happened. They pegged me the most with questions as I was the main one involved in the twisted Romance.

It was a mere hour before dawn in the early summer morning when the police allowed us to return home at last. Pansy felt uneasy with the men walking alone after the event. Too tired to worry about the scandal, we invited them in and all collapsed on the couches in our family room.

Stacy was rightly startled when she woke up to two men in our dormitory, wondering when they came in, how long they had been there, more questions, questions, questions. She still knew only the top half of it.

Jake offered to make me breakfast, though he was clueless in our kitchen. Still irritated with him, I offered to assist only as necessary. Pansy and Theo joined us at the dining table.

I grimaced to my roommate. "Maybe I should read that wretched book of yours."

She raised an eyebrow. "Is *Oz's Haunting Survival Book* wretched if it saved my life on multiple accounts and yours this morning? You should probably take a self-defense class too. I think there's a course you can take as a physical education credit."

I struggled to hide my displeasure at the thought of such a class, though I could not argue with the logic. A grueling class would be preferred over repeating that experience.

"How did you know where to find me?" I asked.

Theo smirked. "For a stalker, he failed to recognize when he was being followed. After passing you on the sidewalk, the darkness of your aura worried me. I followed you to his apartment, then called Pansy and the police."

Pansy nodded. "By the time I loaded my gun, I ran into Jake on the way. I didn't invite him, but I said you were in trouble, and he came along."

I turned to Jake. "What are you doing here? Are you not supposed to be in New Angeles?"

My former love shuffled uncomfortably. "I was already planning to come visit you this weekend, after…" He shuffled and did not continue.

Theo frowned. "I never knew Romances could be this dangerous."

Jake's eyebrows bounced upward. "You should read the history of *The Phantom of the Opera*."

"I've read that one!" Pansy shouted with an excited point. Then, seeing all of our bewildered stares, she shrugged. "What? Just because I found it relatable doesn't mean I enjoyed it."

Jake suppressed his laugh to address me. "Heather, I thought you were distantly related to Jane Eyre."

"My great-grandmother on my mother's side was a direct descendant," I said proudly. "However, I always considered Romances to be as safe as a stream." I hugged myself, then glared at Pansy. "I blame your influences."

"Me?" Pansy rocked back. "I'd rather face another werewolf lusting to tear me apart than a creepy stalker lusting for my body."

"Plus," Theo added, "werewolves are often misjudged. Those I know are completely gentle people while in their human forms."

Pansy gave her boyfriend an estranged stare. "What werewolves have you known?"

"Fantastic werewolves, of course," he said. "Most werewolves, witches, wizards, and even some vampires are decent and law-abiding citizens in Fantasy."

Jake and I watched, bemused by the conflicting opinions. It was better than failing to avoid awkward glances with each other.

"So," Pansy pondered, "you're saying Fantasy is a Romantic version of Horror?"

Theo shrugged. "I suppose, in a sense. At least, if this situation had occurred in my homeland, my dictation and delegation would not have been questioned by the local authorities."

Pansy tilted her head to the side. "Are lords like the chief of police in Fantasy?"

"Hardly," Theo laughed. "More appropriately, they are the people whom everyone else trusts to delegate correctly. They recognize that one man cannot do everything, so one man is designated to *delegate* everything. That is why we have land-lords and knights."

Pansy turned away, her eyes speaking of a revelation in her mind. "That sounds almost manageable, I guess."

Theo smiled, and Pansy melted a little more. We all knew Theo's smile was her favorite feature of his.

"Miss Pansy Finster:" he said, "fearless in the face of death. However, the thought of responsibility? Terribly frightful indeed."

We bid Jake and Theo farewell after our stomachs became satisfied with eggs and toast and the sun shone high overhead. My roommate shared a warm and lingering kiss with her boyfriend while I turned to my bedroom with a simple curtsy to Jake. His eyes were pain-stricken and his mouth quivered with a hundred excuses. I wished to hear none of them.

Ensuring that the blinds were closed tightly, I rid myself of my ravished clothes. I changed into a fresh sleeping gown, then crawled into bed for a few hours of blissful sleep.

Chapter 8

I stayed home from church on Sunday and skipped classes on Monday. I had a separate set of classes on Tuesday, allowing me to stay home again without falling too far behind.

Stepping outside was a chore. Opening the blinds was distasteful. I had a full infection of Pansy's paranoia. While I shut out any cracks to the outside world, I blasted every room with every lightbulb possible.

Movies and books were my new favorite distractions. Tried as I might, I could not escape the memories that haunted my sleep or crept into the corners of my thoughts. I escaped into other worlds, into the minds and lives of characters who had different problems.

It was sometime before lunch when a soft knock on my bedroom door startled me from my reading. I was even more surprised when the knocker opened the door slowly, and Pansy revealed herself.

"Hey," she said, holding a bouquet of flowers.

"Who are you, and what have you done to my roommate? Pansy is not one to knock or open the door slowly. And what is that bouquet in your hands?"

Pansy smiled. "I thought I was supposed to be the skeptical one. These are from Jake." She gestured to the small bouquet of lavender flowers. "There's a 'get well' note with them."

"Is there?" I asked without interest. "So much for his compassionate rescue. One moment he offers loving comfort, then he flees back to New Angeles with his scandalous fling. He will need to do a lot better than a mail-order bouquet to convince my forgiveness."

"He didn't return to New Angeles," Pansy said with a frown. "Read the note."

"What?"

Those words at last convinced me to leave the comforts of my bed. I snatched the note from her hands and read it like a person starved for words.

Miss Heather Appleton,
I do hope you feel well enough to venture forth from your chambers soon. My deepest desire is to see you well and to console you from the terrors of that night. However, after our last phone call, I understand if you might not desire to even look on me. Please, when you're able, I wish to apologize properly, face to face.
Please, accept these flowers, that they may reach you where I cannot. May their sweet aroma envelop you as my arms would in fondness.
I pray you may gain the courage to venture out again soon. I would very much like to meet in the campus gardens. Say the word and I'll be there.
Ever yours, Jake.

"'Ever yours,'" I scoffed. "Ever your backstabbing friend is what he meant."

Pansy offered me a sad smile. "Maybe you should return it."

"The flowers?"

"No," she said. "Your cynicism. I hate to say it, but it's my duty as your roommate to tell you when you're wearing something wrong. And, Heather, cynicism doesn't look good on you."

She left without another word, closing the door behind her to leave me alone with my thoughts. They made for unpleasant company.

Unfortunately, I could not persuade myself to throw away his flowered gift. It was full of lavender, my favorite flower for their scent. I buried myself back into bed and my book, though I struggled to concentrate on the story.

Jake had remained in Heartford instead of returning to New Angeles. He was willing to wait as long as it took until I met him again. Brave indeed. He could lose his internship entirely if I kept him waiting too long.

I stewed over his words for longer than I would openly admit. When I came out of my room for a late dinner, Pansy was kind, though it was obvious that she was one counseling couch away from an intervention. When I grabbed multiple desserts, her pointed looks became unbearable.

"Why must you persist?" I burst after my second ice cream sandwich.

She sighed. "Because, as much of an epically failing idiot as he was, he wants to make things right. Even if he doesn't love or deserve you, he cares about you enough to completely drop his internship and forget his dumb new girl to rescue you halfway across the regency. Just talk to him."

I dropped my fork to my plate unceremoniously. "Very well. If that is the requirement for you to leave me alone, then I shall go."

I picked up my handbag and keys, and went to the door. One meter away, however, my body froze.

Who knew what was behind that door? Who knew what eyes would watch for me as soon as I stepped out? Lew had stalked me even in broad daylight. How many others could be lurking in the dimming twilight? Fear gripped my heart, and I stepped back. Pansy wrapped an arm around me.

"Do you want me to go with you? I'll ask Theo to join us."

I caught my breath and nodded. "I would appreciate that, please."

Pansy messaged Theo while I put on my boots. We waited to leave until we received a confirmation message that he and Jake would meet us at the campus gardens. During that time, I simmered my stewing mood and considered my words to the man who played my heart like a flute. Pansy stuffed her emergency pack with her revolver, pepper-spray, flashlight, and taser. For the first time, I appreciated her safety concerns and packed my handbag with my pepper-spray and torchlight before we walked up to campus together.

The campus gardens were ever changing projects for agricultural and landscaping students. This season sported a lovely brick pathway that curved between willow trees and water fountains. It was quite late by the time Pansy and I arrived. The stars shone brightly overhead with a waning, gibbous moon. Theo greeted us at the bottom of the gardens, saying that Jake waited for me near the top. I asked him twice for assurance that my aura manifested no hints of danger.

"I'll keep you in sight," Pansy said, "but we'll be far enough away to give you two privacy." It was the closest phrase to a promise that I had ever heard from her.

She and Theo then parted to roam the garden, while I gathered my courage to head up the pathway, where Jake waited for me under the top gazebo. The columned structure was large enough for a small party, and a plaque claimed its dedication to the Chase Family. Roses hedged upward and entwined with the metal frame as fireflies twinkled in the new night. The picturesque scene was enough to ease my troubled heart.

Standing on opposite sides of the gazebo, Jake greeted me with a nervous smile. "I was unsure if you'd come."

"I was likewise unsure," I said. "You did send me lavender, though. How did you know it was my favorite?"

"You told me as much in the spring. You always commented on their scent as we walked by."

"You remembered? Truly, I was unsure whether you were even listening."

Jake stepped closer, his expression hurt. "Of course I listened to you, Heather. I've talked with you, watched you, I couldn't take my eyes off you. That's why I went on the internship and asked to break up. You were too distracting. I couldn't focus on my school work."

The parallel of his words from Mr. Hunsaker did not escape me. I found it peculiar how different it felt to hear similar phrases from Jake's lips. Instead of frightening, they were endearing. Instead of an announcement of lustful yearning, it was a confession of tender care.

However, it made little sense.

"What about your kiss with your fellow intern?"

Jake sighed. "That shouldn't have happened. What would you have me say? Is there anything I can say that will help you forgive me?"

"No."

"Well, I'm sorry."

"As you should be," I scoffed. "Regardless of what you say, I cannot trust you because actions speak louder than words."

His face fell. "Would you have me quit my internship? Say the word, and I'll stay here with you."

A part of me wanted to say yes. I wanted to test his loyalty and his word if he truly meant the offer. I also wanted him to stay in Heartford, away from New Angeles and away from the woman he kissed.

No. Real love was not spiteful.

"No, Jake. Your education is important. If you wish to regain my trust, I need an honest explanation. After some thought, I have come to realize that what bothers me is not the fact that you kissed a woman despite your promise not to court anyone while in New Angeles. Or—fine, it does bother me that you broke your promise, but even more so, you neglected to tell me. Why did you keep secrets from me? We talked on the phone, and you said nothing of it! I had to learn of it from Pansy, through Hank, from some social media post that you announced to the world!"

He cringed. "The woman I kissed—a fellow intern—found my laptop open and created the post. I deleted it as soon as I noticed the next day and left her to come here. I hoped you wouldn't learn about it since you don't use social media, but I came to apologize in person… Oh gosh, Pansy knows? Please, don't let her kill me."

"I have half the mind," I said. "Did you do something to offend her, also?"

"Not exactly," he said, shrinking. "Only that, when we first started courting, she told me that if I broke your heart, she'd break my face."

I was inclined to believe Jake's word and my roommate's capabilities on that matter.

"I never wanted to hurt you," he said. "I'm sorry. I broke my promise then lied about it because I was ashamed. You deserve better."

He continued to talk with slow and incremental footsteps towards me, as if each footfall agonized him.

190

"I am sorry, Heather. I got caught up in the moment and hoped she'd help me forget about you, but I could only think of how I'd hurt you. I came to make things right, but then Pansy ran into me, saying you were in danger. I couldn't stand the thought of someone hurting you. I had to help, even if I didn't know how. I wouldn't rest until you were safe. I stayed here regardless of your silence, because I wanted to be here for you when you broke that silence…" He paused in his approach, within arm's reach. "Because without you, nothing else has meaning."

A sob escaped my mouth before I could turn away. Oh, how my heart yearned for him. My brain blurted without censorship, "I still love you, too."

Fool of a woman! Was I so desperate to make myself look weak and hormonal?

"That…wasn't what I said," he whispered. "But it's true."

I turned back around, tears shining in my eyes. "Your actions spoke louder."

He had left the woman and any possibilities of a relationship, plus extended his leave from his internship, risking his career for me.

A timid smile lifted his lips as he searched my face. Then, a painful thought shifted his expression. "I waited too long."

"For what?"

"To kiss you. Will you forgive me for giving my first to another? It was a stupid mistake, but…I couldn't kiss you before. I was too scared. Because I knew the moment we kissed…there'd be no stopping my fall for you."

My mind whirled with a million thoughts and emotions. Oh, my word—dear heavens—no—wait—maybe?—except… Memories of that horrible night attacked me, and I flinched.

"But now…" He frowned. "That wretched man hurt you in one of the worst ways. He took an experience that's supposed to be beautiful and poisoned it. I want to kiss you, Heather, but I promise not to push against your will."

Already, there was no comparison between Mr. Hunsaker's abuse and Jake's tenderness. Did I still want Jake's kiss? Could his honest love wash away the trauma of lust?

Jake shuffled shyly. "I don't expect you to forgive me right away…but please let me be with you to help you while you heal and…maybe be something more than we were before."

Finding my courage, I said, "I think that I may like that. And, perhaps…" I raised my fingertips to his jaw and dared to draw him closer. His eyes widened with surprise before he squeezed them shut, holding himself back from doing anything more than reacting to my touch.

Could I actually kiss him? I had dreamed about this moment for months. It wasn't during a holiday, or in the rain, or any other of my daydream situations, but…I had wanted Jake's kiss before Mr. Hunsaker tainted the experience. The night stars twinkled overhead as we stood under the shelter of the gazebo surrounded by beautiful flowers.

Only with the gentle press of my lips against his did I relax. Then, I did more than relax; I melted. My anger steamed off, my cynicism rolled down, and my insecurities pushed away. I became a liquid, and the only thing holding me together was Jake's arms.

The differences between Mr. Hunsaker's and Jake's kisses were so vast, they did not even relate. In that blissful moment, the attack was forgotten with the sweetness of this new moment that I wanted to remember forever. Jake's lips caressed mine with a feathery touch, then pulled back all too soon. To my embarrassment, I leaned in again like a drunk asking for one more sip.

"Oh gosh," he whispered, pulling my attention. "I was right about that fall."

My smile cracked, releasing a full flush on my cheeks. I giggled, filling my lungs after Jake's breathtaking kiss.

Nightmarish memories crept in the shadows of my less-naïve mind, but with Jake standing with me and his tender love, I had hope for a brighter future.

Acknowledgements

Thank YOU, dear readers, for your encouragement and enthusiasm for these characters and settings in Novel. Thank you for reading all the way to the end, and an extra thank you to those who leave honest and kind reviews.

For being more than your usual awesome Alpha Reader, thank you, Robyn Cheatham. Thanks for putting up with me as a roommate and for putting up with the situation that inspired Heather's novelette. Yes, I changed it drastically to make Jake easier to forgive. May we forever celebrate Epic Fail Day with cheap pizzas, mint ice cream, and "Hitch" or "She's the Man."

A large piece of my gratitude goes to Jim Doran, who was promoted (demoted?) to an Alpha Reader with this collection because of his own experience with writing short story collections and his consistently insightful suggestions. Seriously, I laugh how we have the same story-brain. Readers, if you enjoy my stories, look him up, because every time we share a manuscript with each other, the other says, "I have a story like that."

I'd also like to thank my Beta Readers: Hannah Bridgeman, Bettilee Hunt, Colleen Dowda, Rachel Spaeth, and NaDell Ransom.

As always, my last (but far from least) thanks go to Michael and God. Michael, not only do you meet my tight reading deadlines (despite my stories not being "your genre"), you suffer through the worst of spoilers as I bounce my ideas off of you. Thank you for being my number one supporter. I love you for all eternity.

Then, thank you, God, for messing up my head just enough to give me ideas, but not too much so others can enjoy them too.

About the Author

C. Rae D'Arc has been involved in every stage of a book's life. As a writer, editor, retailer, reader, and reviewer, she once worked four part-time jobs simultaneously. Thankfully, one of them actually paid her. She received her Bachelors in English from Brigham Young University, and now lives in the Tri-Cities of Washington with her husband and Aussie dog.

Follow C. Rae D'Arc on
Facebook: https://www.facebook.com/c.rae.darc/
Instagram: https://www.instagram.com/craedarc/

Read more about her books on https://craedarc.com/

PS. To save you from hiccups, D'Arc only has one syllable.